I0628092

updated April 11, 2015
54634 words

THE GOLD CHROMOSOME

A Mystery by

Harley L. Sachs

Harley L. Sachs

This is a work of fiction. Any resemblance to people living or dead is coincidental and unintentional. None of my family are in this.

ISBN 1939381126

ISBN 978-1-939381-12-5

Books by Harley L. Sachs:

Novels

Queer Company
Never Trust a Talking Horse
The Gold Chromosome
Murder by Mail (Scratch—out!)!
Ben Zakkai's Coffin
The Search for Jesse Bram
The Mystery Club Solves a Murder
The Mystery Club and the Dead Doctor
The Mystery Club and the Hidden Witness
The Mystery Club and the Serial Widow
Conspiracy!
Murder in the Keweenaw
The Lollipop Murder
Betrayal
Retribution
Burnt Out
White Slave
Sam in Love
StopRape.com
The Accidental Courier

Collections of short fiction

Ahoy! Quarterdeck! (Irma Quarterdeck Reports)
Anna-Lena's Troll and other stories
Threads of the Covenant: The Jews of Red Jacket
Misplaced Persons

Non-Fiction

Freelance Non-Fiction Articles
    The Misadventures of Cpl. Sachs
    The 1957 Sachs Arctic Expedition
    From Tent to Castle: Memoir of a Year-Long Honeymoon
    IS
Chilly-Chilly BANG! How We Freelanced Through Europe's Coldest
        Winter in a VW with a Kid
    Essays and Columns: 1992-2011
    The Writing Life

Cartoons

Hunting the Mail Buoy and other hazards to navigation

Dedicated to the memory of Uncle Sam Sachs the cab driver who was murdered for twenty-four dollars, Aunt Betty Diamond, and to all the cousins who stand to inherit from Betty's estate.

Thanks to my wife Ulla and to Art Anderson for their insightful comments and corrections, to my brother Charles Sachs, James Jenkins, and those who reviewed the draft of the book and made constructive comments and suggestions.

The Back Story

Gold was not our mother's original family name. It was something Russian and, unless you're a Slav, unpronounceable. Great grandfather Isaac, so the family legend goes, had the chutzpah to steal a horse from a drunken Cossack and flee to Poland. He kept running westward and landed in England where he settled among the Russian Jewish immigrants in London's east end. I think he had a push cart -- no horse-- in Petticoat Lane where you're likely to have your pocket picked.

Great Grandpa's having stolen a Cossack's horse seems to have set the pattern for the whole family, for though they may not be horse thieves, the Golds are brassy, conniving and crooked, sometimes even criminal.

Great Grandpa Isaac had several children but only Abe emigrated to America. Times were always tough in the East End, so as soon as Abe could he got a steerage passage to the United States. His first act upon arrival at Ellis Island was to change his name to Gold. He'd heard that in America the streets were paved with it, and he wanted to get off on the right foot.

Grandpa Abe Gold was only fourteen, claimed to be sixteen, and got to Chicago where he started as a runner, carrying numbers for gangsters. Eventually Abe had his own news stand in the Loop. Until I learned the true nature of grandpa Gold's business, I always wondered how someone could move from Hyde Park on the South Side and retire to such a fine house in Deerfield and drive a Cadillac on what he earned selling copies of the *Chicago Tribune*, the *Sun Times*, and a few magazines.

Abe Gold married and had six children, all of whom grew up while the family still lived in Hyde Park. Ann Gold Rottman, my mother of blessed memory, was somewhere in the middle of the brood and Sadie was the youngest. Naturally, there are lots of cousins. Those were the days before television and birth control. Besides my mother and Sadie there were... well, let me get to that later. I'll introduce them as we go along, and I guarantee you won't be disappointed. Trust me. Trust-- that's a family joke.

1. Sitting Shiva

You know how it is with funerals. Relatives who are seldom in touch and may not be on speaking terms gather to pay their final respects. Sadie was the youngest of the Gold family, one of six children on my mother's side, the last of her generation. She made it to her ninety-third birthday, had a stroke, and that was it, dead.

Some of the cousins still live in the Chicago area and my home is in Michigan. Not everyone made it to the funeral. My brother Harold refused. Not that he had anything against Aunt Sadie. He didn't want to be in the same room with the cousins, even for a funeral. When our mother of blessed memory was dying of cancer, none of the cousins showed any interest. They didn't come to her funeral and had the chutzpah to ask if they were in her will. Harold never forgave them.

Those who did show up for Aunt Sadie's funeral gathered in Sarah's cluttered living room. So there we were, I, my weird sister Sarah, and three other cousins at Sarah's crazy apartment in North Hollywood.

The funeral people had provided Sarah with a Shiva candle, the kind that burn for the seven day period of mourning. We're not Orthodox, so we don't spend seven days in darkened rooms in our stocking feet with the mirrors covered. Others are supposed to bring in food so you don't have to cook while you contemplate the loss of your loved one and say prayers.

There was a silent moment while we watched Sarah light the Shiva candle and set it on the mantelpiece to celebrate or mourn the passing of Aunt Sadie.

Cluttered is a euphemism. Sarah may be pushing sixty but she never got over the Raggedy Ann doll stage. She has hundreds of those rag dolls piled everywhere in her apartment, staring with those blank, trusting, painted on black eyes, enough to fill a museum.

She even dresses like Raggedy Ann, wears her hair in braids, though her braids are gray, and wears an apron and red and white striped stockings. Sarah's eyes are gray, too, unlike Raggedy Ann's. Sometimes she has that blank look like Dan Quayle.

Sarah never goes anywhere without one of those damned dolls. It's her obsession. There's a miniature Raggedy Ann dangling from the rear view mirror of Sarah's Lady Bug orange, vintage Volkswagen. Look in her commodious shoplifter's purse and I'll bet there's a Raggedy Andy hiding in there. It's her dream to sell her collection to the Getty Museum for a million bucks and retire. She has two problems with that: 1) she could never part with those dolls and 2) the Getty Museum is interested in real art. A possible third reason is that there's already a Raggedy Ann museum in the midwest.

Aside from trading in dolls, Sarah used to almost earn a living photographing bar and bat mitzvahs. Videographers do that now, preserving the proverbial "today I am a man" speeches forever on videotape. Sarah has an aversion to such newfangled media, asserting correctly that they are not as archival as her own black and white prints. Trouble is, no one wants black and white still photos of bar mitzvahs these days.

She is not averse to computers and the internet, and is forever trading on eBay, searching for that rare doll not yet in her collection and sometimes selling off the duplicates. She buys and sells under the pseudonym Mamadoll. Memorabilia is her shtick. Collecting is her disease.

Our older brother Harold is her benefactor. Collecting dolls and taking bar mitzvah pictures doesn't pay the rent. Harold does. "She my baby sister," he told me once, even though, like I said before, she's almost sixty.

Gathered in Sarah's cluttered space to mourn Aunt Sadie, you wouldn't know Sarah even had a computer, for it was almost buried in the dinette under a pile of staring dolls.

So there we were, the five cousins who made it to the funeral plus one spouse, gathered at Sarah's place, comparing notes about Aunt Sadie, the last of her generation. Making it to ninety-three means good genes, not necessarily good quality of life. Her life had ended, but not her story. For me, it was the beginning.

As for the late Aunt Sadie, whom I hadn't seen in years, my recollection was of a fragile old lady with blue hair and a limp. I do remember that she had a reputation of never picking up the check at lunch. There's a story of her trying to take home the carcass of a thanksgiving turkey in a doggy bag when she visited my mother, she should rest in peace. Imagine asking to take home not just a doggie bag, but half a turkey! Sadie had that Gold chromosome: chutzpah. That's how I remember her. It's a one-sided memory at best.

"She had a tough time of it in the end," my sister Sarah said as she passed around a tray of Mogan David HD wine for a kiddush blessing. That Raggedy Ann apron and striped stockings made her look like a waitress in some theme restaurant, not our hostess. "I couldn't get her to pay her bills. She'd just put them away in a drawer."

I took a glass of wine. "Too cheap to pay her bills? Sounds like Sadie."

"No," Sarah corrected, looking at me from under her unkempt, gray bangs, "Just didn't want to be bothered. Didn't want to sweat the details. That's why I was given power of attorney. I took over paying her bills. Didn't want her phone to be cut off. Not that she made any calls herself. If they cut off her phone, how could I reach her?"

My cousin Schmuel, schlemiel to my mind, took a glass of wine off the tray and chugged it down before we got to the blessing. He's one of those Californians who wears his sunglasses indoors. At least they're plain dark, not the asinine reflective kind. Schmuel got his start standing on street corners hawking maps to the homes of the stars. Later he sometimes worked as an extra at Universal so considers himself part of "the industry." In California that means the movie business, what else? Schmuel licked his lips. "So you got power of attorney. Who set that up?"

Sarah was reluctant to say. She took a deep breath, looked away, and admitted, "Harold."

Schmuel gave us both a suspicious look. "Your brother the lawyer? How convenient for you."

"Nobody else in the family was willing to help her out. She told me that when she needed someone to take her shopping you were always too busy."

Schmuel shrugged. "I got business to attend to. So what about Sadie's estate, since you're privy to inside information? Any money there?"

"Yes," his wife Sylvia put in. Some people would call her Schmuel's trophy wife, but to me she's just a braless, dyed brunette shicksa who married Schmuel thinking he had money because he drove a Lexus. Schmuel has a thing for expensive, flashy cars. Maybe Schmuel did have money once, before he lost it in one of his schemes or Sylvia got hold of his credit cards. "So are we going to inherit?"

Sarah wasn't saying.

"I bet she had plenty," Schmuel said. "She never spent any of it." He paused to reflect. "Those jokes she'd tell! You're never believe the language that came out of her mouth."

Up to now my cousin Millie was quiet. Millie lived a couple of blocks away from Sadie's old apartment on Fairfax. Millie's husband had been self employed but never paid any income tax, so when he died his social security didn't help Millie much. What little money he left her got eaten up by Millie's medical bills years ago. Like Sarah, she lived on food stamps and was lucky to be in rent controlled housing. She didn't drive, never owned a car. As a widow Millie supplemented her social security by working part time at a Good Will store as a cashier. That explains why everything she wore was no longer in style. Millie's wardrobe was the opposite of Schmuel's wife's. Sylvia wears stuff manufactured with the labels on the outside for status.

Cousin Millie agreed. "We were crossing Fairfax once when a driver tried to drive through the zebra crossing with her in it. Some guy with a big Mercedes. Sadie whacked a dent in his hood with her cane and when he got out of the car to confront her she told him he was a stupid motherfucking Nazi trying to run down old ladies in the crosswalk. 'Piss off before I call the cops!' she said. You should have seen the look on his face. The guy fled."

I never expected modest and self-deprecating Cousin Millie to come out with language like that, even quoting Sadie. This family is full of surprises. Whacking a Mercedes with her cane? Clearly that wasn't the Aunt Sadie I knew, but then I didn't know her. I live in Lansing, Michigan, thousands of miles from LA, so had no opportunity to protect drivers from Aunt Sadie's mouth or her cane when crossing Fairfax.

Schmuel had done Sadie's memory the honor of putting on a shirt with collar and sleeves as a sign of respect. Not the usual California style where tee shirts, shorts and sandals are the uniform. By contrast, Jake Gold, my cousin from Chicago, was the only one who came to the funeral in a suit. Jake, a little guy with a paunch, wore a navy blue, pin stripe, three piece Italian business suit to give himself a look of respectability and shoulder pads to make him look bigger than he is. Fortunately, the shirt wasn't black and the tie not white satin like you might expect on someone like him. His shoes looked like they were elevated to give him a couple more inches.

What you notice about Jake is not what he wears, but how he wears it. Jake has a sort of swagger, the demeanor you see in cops and police detectives, or on made Mafia men. There's no proof, but it's common knowledge in the family that Jake is a gangster. We all know that "Mafia Man" Jake is the only one in the family who, like our late Grandpa Abe, has a news stand in the Chicago Loop. Same business and it ain't just newspapers and dirty magazines. Jake said, "If you think she had a foul mouth, did you ever play cards with her?"

None of us had. I had heard Sadie played fan tan with her pals in the nursing home where she lived the last two years of her life, but I had never played cards with her myself.

Jake had more to tell. "I used to play casino with her when I was a kid, before Uncle Dave was killed and she moved to LA. She'd cheat."

"Cheat?" my sister Sarah asked.

"Yeh." Jake was still holding his full glass of Mogan David HD. "Are we doing a blessing or what?"

We all raised our glasses, praised God and thanked Him for the fruit of the vine and drank to Aunt Sadie's memory.

"Eat something," Sarah insisted. She had put out a tray of distressed bagels that had languished for God knows how long in her freezer. She had smeared them with a little cream cheese, but nobody wanted to eat the proceeds of Sarah's food stamps.

Jake returned to his story. "Imagine cheating a little kid at casino. She had this dishonest streak."

What did Jake care about dishonesty? "Runs in the family, maybe?" I said, remembering the family history.

Jake didn't smile. He gave me one of those looks meant for people who deserved to be dead, soon. "Ever know why she moved to LA? How Uncle Dave came to be killed?"

I searched my memory. Family business gets pretty complicated and the stories blur. Each time they're told someone embellishes the truth for greater effect. Maybe the stories blur because they're just rumors and malicious gossip. "No. I think he was in the used car business."

Jake returned his now empty wine glass to Sarah's tray. His fingers hesitated over a little dish of candy hearts with the caption "I love you" just like the hearts in the chests of Raggedy Ann and Andy. Jake popped one in his mouth and talked around it. "Used cars is a euphemism. Dave was in the hot car business. He'd get a few stolen Caddies, forge the bills of sale, and sell them on time payments at high interest to the schwarzes."

Schwarze is no longer politically correct Yiddish. The translation is "black" but the negative connotations are the same as "nigger."

"Dave knew the schwarzes could never keep up the payments, so when they'd miss he'd simply repossess the cars and sell them again to some other suckers." Jake paused, crunched the candy heart and swallowed. "One day one of his customers got lucky. Won big in a back alley crap game, and came in with a buddy to pay Dave off in cash. Wanted the title to the car. Dave didn't have a title."

Now Jake had a tight circle of cousins all listening, rapt. It's a long way from Chicago to LA. Schmuel's wife Sylvia, for sure, hadn't heard this story. I hadn't, either.

Jake gave us his humorless smile. "So Dave takes out his gun, kills 'em both, puts them in the trunk of the Caddy, and drives it into the canal by the old steel mill in Gary." He chuckled. Obviously to Jake killing schwarzes is funny.

I knew there was something shady about my uncle Dave's car business, but I didn't know it involved murder. There was more.

"Everything was OK for awhile, but some of the schwarzes' friends from the crap game knew they were headed for Dave's car lot and got suspicious. He'd bumped off the wrong guys. So one day when Dave doesn't show up for supper and doesn't answer the phone Sadie drives down to the South Side to see what's up and finds him all tied up, dead. They cut his throat."

"What a shock for Sadie," I said. "Must have been a sight."

Jake caught my grimace. "That ain't the half. First they took down his pants and gave him a second circumcision. They cut his cock off."

I shuddered at the description. "You sure they weren't Arabs?" I asked. "Sounds like something Arabs would do." I remembered stories of Arabs cutting off a victim's penis and stuffing it into his navel, which I guessed was making someone into a motherfucker. Obscure acts of symbolic mutilation elude me. I'd have to ask Deborah, my wife the psychologist. She'd know. "So Sadie left Chicago and moved to LA," I said, thinking that was the end to the story.

"Not Sadie," Jake said, his expression cool and tired. "First she put out a contract on the guys who did it. As payment she handed the business over to the people who furnished the cars and split."

The amazing thing about this story wasn't that Sadie had put out a contract for murder, but that my cousins weren't horrified or even much surprised. Maybe we live with so much murder and mayhem that we're no longer shocked by anything. Deborah would call it a double standard, that the cousins would have been upset if the victims were Jewish, not black.

I doubted the story. "How do you know all this?"

This time Jake's smile was genuine. "Some of my business associates are familiar with the details."

Schmuel complained that Sarah had provided no better than Mogen David, but refilled his wine glass anyway. "I thought you Mafia types took the code of silence."

Jake shrugged. He had unbuttoned the vest of his three piece suit. "It was a long time ago. The principals are all dead. Besides, this is family business." He nodded at Sarah's four walls.

After waiting patiently for a break in the conversation Millie spoke. "I always thought Sadie was a sweet old thing. I used to go over to her place for coffee. I'd get some day old pastry at the deli and we'd sit on the balcony and visit. She knew everybody. She also never forgot if you did her wrong. She had a grudge against the landlord, but that's a long story I won't go into." She paused as if considering whether the next subject was appropriate. "So are we going to inherit anything? She lived so poor, there can't be anything to her estate."

12

Sarah had told me that when Sadie moved into the nursing home she had phoned Millie and given her Sadie's microwave, television, coffee pot, and what remained of the better dishes. A few possessions and some worn out furniture wasn't much of an accumulation after ninety years.

Sarah hesitated, not knowing what to say or if she should say anything at all.

Schmuel insisted. "I hear Sadie left a chunk of money. Who gets it?"

Sarah collected the empty wine glasses and put down the tray before she explained. "Sadie's assets were put into an irrevocable trust. Harold set it up."

"Dear cousin Harold," Schmuel said, his voice dripping with suspicion. He looked at me. "Why didn't your brother come for the funeral?"

I could have said my brother Harold is too fat. At over three hundred pounds he has to fly first class or they can't wedge him into a seat on the plane. "Got a big case," I explained. Harold is the oldest of the Rottmans and the brains of our side of the family. His law practice is in Indianapolis. Mom was a Gold, of course, but she married a Rottman. Considering the prejudice Jews of German extraction hold against Russian and Polish Jews, marrying a Rottman was a step up in the world. Of course, being Rottmans doesn't mean we didn't inherit the Gold chromosome.

Sarah relented and explained. "Too bad he couldn't come to the funeral to explain all this himself. That legal stuff is beyond me. I do understand that you're all to get a few hundred dollars as a token."

Schmuel was puzzled. "What about you?"

Sarah was embarrassed. "The interest from the trust fund goes to me while I'm alive."

"And then?" Schmuel asked, licking his lips and looking at her over the top of his sunglasses as if to assess how soon her demise might be.

"Then it's to be split among the cousins... I think."

Schmuel was counting. "That's us in this room, Harold, crazy Arthur in Calumet city, and his ditsy sister what's her name?"

"Miriam," I said. "The one married to a butcher with the two kids."

Sylvia wasn't counting relatives. She was figuring how long Sarah could live before she died and the rest of us divided up Sophie's estate. She protested. "We could all be dead by then!"

Jake shrugged. "You never know." To Sarah he added, "You got life insurance?" It sounded like a threat.

Sarah didn't take it as a bad joke. "For who should I buy life insurance? Who would collect? Raggedy Ann and Andy?"

Schmuel checked out the collection. "Make me your beneficiary. I heard this stuff is valuable. These must be worth a bundle." He picked up a doll from the pile that cluttered the couch.

"Hands, off, Schmuel."

I could feel the tension rising in the room. The Gold cousins. Not a pretty lot. Maybe it's a good thing we're not close.

So that was my reintroduction to Aunt Sadie: a little old lady who wouldn't spend a penny, who drank coffee with cousin Millie on the balcony, Sadie who cheated at cards, wasn't afraid of drivers who encroached on zebra crossings, and was capable of putting out a contract for murder. Next time I see a little old gal with blue hair, tennis shoes and sunglasses with rhinestones I'll give her extra respect. Maybe that's why the street thugs never grab their shopping bags. Hit a bag lady and you're soon dead.

2. Tontine

"Why don't we call Harold in Indianapolis and tell him the funeral went off OK?" I suggested to Sarah. "Where's your phone?"

Sarah searched under the dolls and found her Rolodex with the number. The five of us squeezed into the dinette while she dialed. Jake tried to keep his pin stripe suit from brushing against the stove. I don't think Sarah ever cleaned it and she does a lot of frying. One of these days that stove could ignite and Raggedy Ann and Andy would be toast.

"I hope we don't just get his voice mail," Sarah said.

Schmuel sneered. "Big shot lawyer, you'd expect that."

We were lucky. She got through. "Harold? It's Sarah."

All we could hear at our end was a little squeak from the receiver. Too bad she didn't have a speaker phone. Sarah's part of the conversation consisted mainly of "Yes, yeh, sure," and "Arthur and Miriam couldn't come. He's afraid to leave his business in Calumet City. Millie, Schmuel and his wife, Jake, Adam and I are here."

Adam, that's me, even though I wasn't the number one son. At least they didn't name us Cain and Abel, though considering the reputation of the Golds that might have been appropriate. We're not Golds, I keep reminding myself. We're Rottmans. Gold is my mother's family. That's my alibi and I'm sticking to it.

Millie surprised me by hustling the phone from Sarah. "Harold!" Suddenly her demeanor was all sweetness. She carried on about poor Aunt Sadie but couldn't bring herself to what everyone wanted to know.

"Gimme that phone," Schmuel said. "Let's cut to the chase."

Hollywood talk, I thought to myself. This is Los Angeles. They speak a language of their own here.

"What's this about Sarah living off the interest until she dies?" Schmuel demanded.

The phone receiver made little squeaky sounds.

"Just how much is the estate worth?"

Another squeak.

Schmuel whistled. "Would I believe four million? No shit? I'd never have thought it." He looked at the cousins. "He says would I believe four million bucks?"

Exclamations all around. "Four million! We're rich!" Jubilation. Et cetera.

I protested. "That's not possible. I don't believe it."

Jake was attentive. "I would. I heard she never spent a dime. Must have kept it under her mattress."

"Wait!" Schmuel signaled, holding up one finger. "What? What's that?" Schmuel turned to us, angry. "He says it's not four million. He says would we believe one million."

"Four million, one schmillion, so what?" Millie said. "Even with one sixth of that I could pay off that hospital bill, get some new clothes instead of these schmates." She pointed to her Good Will wardrobe.

Another squeak on the phone.

Jake wrested the receiver from Schmuel with a deft twist like he was disarming a mugger. "This is Jake. Hi, Harold. One million or four million? OK, one million. That would pay my mortgage, even if I got one sixth of it." Jake paused, listening. "Explain. What list? A what? A tontine? What's a tontine?"

Jake almost dropped the phone and looked at all of us in turn. "A tontine. All the money goes to the last survivor on the list. The whole million."

I'm not the type to wish someone dead. "Thank goodness I don't need the money."

"The last survivor?" Sylvia looked at each of us, assessing our ability to outlive the others.

"But that could take years," Millie protested, despairing. She could use more than the token few hundred bucks Sarah had mentioned.

"Let me talk to him," I said and took the phone from Jake whose hold was now limp. "Harold?"

Harold was wheezing. Besides being fat he has emphysema. A guy like that could die from laughing. "A tontine, Adam. They'll be watching each other like snakes looking for lunch. Don't eat any meals with the cousins. You never know what they'll put in the food." He laughed again like he would choke.

A tontine. Dear Aunt Sadie was more perverse than I suspected. Cheating at cards or bashing Mercedes was nothing. Even ordering a hit on a couple of killers was child's play. A tontine would pit everyone in the Gold family against all the rest. "If I had a medal I'd give it to Aunt Sadie," I said. "This is the ultimate in the Gold chromosome."

I was reconciled to living on my pension, even though my wife is still working, but I wasn't prepared to be on the list of Gold cousins standing in the way of the last survivor's inheritance. As a Rottman I have a live and let live attitude. As a Gold, I'm not confident the others are so tolerant. Greed is a terrible thing.

My cousins were all family but we were never close and I seldom saw them. Now I was beginning to be afraid to have anything to do with any of them.

Millie said Sadie bore grudges. I could see that she might put a hit on whoever murdered my uncle, but what did she have against us? That I didn't send her a birthday or Hanukah card? It looked like my aunt had set us up for war.

3. A farewell gift

Harold's setting up Sadie's estate got rid of his financial responsibility for Sarah. With Sarah getting the interest, he wouldn't have to pay her rent. If something happened to Harold, Sarah wouldn't become a bag lady pushing a shopping cart full of Raggedy Ann dolls. She could go on making deals on eBay and drive her elderly Volkswagen down to Trader Joes for coupon deals.

Sarah had no spare bed in her cluttered apartment so I stayed the night at a motel nearby, kept awake by rowdy drunks in the room next door.

I had a morning flight for my return to Michigan. Sarah picked me up at my motel carrying a paper plate of leftovers from the Shiva party "so I wouldn't have to go out for breakfast" and drove me out to LAX. My suitcase didn't fit under the hood and had to be squeezed into the back seat with a bunch of junk. I sat with the plate of recycled bagels, the cream cheese now dried out, and pretended to eat breakfast while she drove.

California is supposed to be the land of sunshine. They used to joke about people retiring to California to be with their parents. Now in the best of days there's a yellow pall over LA. This was not the best of days. The sky was dark. Sarah said the guy on the weather channel warned of heavy rain and local flooding. Though often dry, when it does rain in Los Angeles you can be swept down a storm drain in the act of stepping out of your car. I was glad to escape the city before it arrived.

For all her experience, Sarah was not a very competent driver with that stick shift. Either that or the clutch just naturally slipped. She's also a slow driver, the bane of freeway drivers. If someone honks the horn at her she flips him off. This is not a safe thing to do in LA where so many drivers are armed and angry. The

Volkswagen's muffler was bad, so I didn't try to carry on a conversation on our way to the airport.

I just sat, scared, watching the miniature doll that dangled from the rear view mirror and wishing the VW had air bags. On the freeway full of SUVs and trucks driven by uninsured Mexicans without licenses life in an aging Volkswagen can be short, the ending not happy.

Sarah dropped me off at LAX curbside. "You don't mind if I don't go to the gate, do you?" she asked. "I hate to pay that parking."

"No problem." I left the paper plate on the seat and extricated my bag from the back.

"Let me give you something," Sarah said, and pressed upon me a Raggedy Andy. It had the battered look of a doll much loved by some kid a long time before the inevitable garage sale.

I didn't conceal my anguish. "A doll?"

"It's valuable," she said. "For luck." She blew me a kiss.

So that's how I came to be sheepishly schlepping my suitcase through LAX with a Raggedy Andy doll under my arm. Fortunately I realized that among the weirdoes and the freaks that pass through Los Angeles, a senior citizen with his dolly on his arm was of no interest to anyone.

At the check-in the airline clerk was in her thirties, weary of confronting belligerent travelers whose flights are delayed or canceled. She went through the routine, demanding to see a picture ID. I showed her. "Did you pack your bag yourself? Are you carrying anything as a convenience for someone else?"

"Just this doll my sister gave me," I said, trying to be cute. "Andy went through the Xray machine. Nothing inside him but a candy heart." I hoped.

Thinking back on the funeral party, I wouldn't have been so confident if the gift had come from Schmuel or, worse, Jake. Even with loss of purchasing power through inflation, one million dollars is still a lot of money. If the doll had come from Jake it might have been one of those that talk when you pull the string. Pull the string and boom. One less cousin.

Of course, the tontine didn't come into play as long as Sarah was alive. She was in good health. For the time being at least, I had nothing to worry about.

4. Lansing

By the time I changed planes in Detroit I was tired and hungry. I'd asked for a kosher meal and they served me a frozen corned beef sandwich. I sent it back and it came back scorched on the outside, but still frozen inside.

Aunt Sadie's funeral and the cousins were far away. Now that the estate would provide Sarah with an income, she'd no longer risk becoming a street person. Though I was never foolish enough to lend Sarah money, her new independence was a load off my mind.

It was raining in Lansing and cold. No palm trees or people running around in shorts with headsets. I found my aging Volvo station wagon in the long term lot at the Lansing airport. The battery was weak. At first I thought it would peter out before the engine caught. The right front tire looked low but I made it to a service station. I was back to reality, my life as a house spouse. Since I retired I'm the cook and have even learned how to do laundry, though ironing is not my most proficient skill.

My wife Deborah still has her practice. She's a psychologist. Didn't have the ambition to do medical school or the money for the costly preparation for psychiatry. Studying psychology at Michigan State promised more job opportunities than sociology. Deborah still has a sixties attitude that grew out of protesting the Vietnam war. There's no money in being an old hippy. Instead of marching and sticking flowers into the muzzles of national guardsmen's rifles Deborah's now active in the League of Women voters.

Having two kids and moving up to a size fourteen didn't make Deborah any less attractive. She's just more squeezable. The gray in her hair gives her that desirable look of what the French call a woman of a certain age-- experienced, but not too old to appreciate sex and the other good things in life.

I was famished when I got home. After Deborah's welcoming squeeze I went to the fridge. Nearly empty. "You didn't shop?" I protested. "There's nothing in here but..." I opened the lid of an old whipped topping container. "...looks like some old stir fry."

"Let's eat out," Deborah suggested. She gave me her "I'm too tired to cook and besides it's your job" look. "Then you can tell me about the funeral without having to run to the kitchen to check something on the stove."

I thought of one of those JAP jokes: "How does a Jewish American Princess do dinner? She tells the kids to get in the car," but I thought the better of it. I didn't feel like cooking, either.

At the Olive Garden in East Lansing we warmed up with the house red wine, the fresh baked bread, and the refillable salad as I told the story of Sadie's funeral and the tontine.

"Your dear old Aunt Sadie had a perverse sense of humor," Deborah said as she picked a pepper from her salad and set it aside. "Either that or your lawyer brother Harold has a mischievous streak. A tontine? If this were a mystery story I'd wonder who would die first. You better watch your back, Adam." She was only half joking.

"As long as Sarah is alive I have nothing to worry about," I said, "and she's the youngest of the three Rottmans."

"Then let's hope she has a long life," Deborah said. There was still some wine in her glass. "Lechaim!"

"To life!" Little did I know.

5. A Drowning

It was no shock when Aunt Sadie died. She was ninety-three. But a chill ran up my spine when I got a call from brother Harold. "You'd better fly back to LA. There's been an accident. Sarah's missing."

In my wild imagination I pictured my sister Sarah being snatched by some of greedy cousin Jake's business associates and... I didn't want to go there. "What happened?"

Harold was careful with his choice of words. Lawyers do that, like everything you say will be transcribed and show up in the appeals court. "Her car went into the Los Angeles river."

Los Angeles actually does have a river. It's boxed in between high concrete walls like an irrigation ditch and is dry most of the year, but when it rains in LA or in the mountains above, the floods can be awesome. People stepping out of their parked cars have been known to be swept away. The current in the otherwise empty Los Angeles concrete channel is unbelievable. I saw a newsreel once showing some crazy kid who tied a rope to a bridge railing and water skied on that flood. Others haven't been so lucky. Three skateboarders got surprised when a flash flood caught them. Two drowned. The TV coverage was a thrilling diversion for Angelinos used to watching real life car chases on the freeways.

"What happened?" I asked, horrified at the thought of Sarah trapped in her aging Volkswagen and being swept out to the Pacific.

Harold explained, "It looks like she took a wrong turn. Apparently it was raining so hard that the water looked like a wet street. The car was swept downstream quite a ways."

"What about Sarah?"

"No sign of her," Harold said. "Her body could be out in the ocean. I'm afraid she's dead."

"Not necessarily." Despairing, I searched for some less fatal scenarios. "Someone might have stolen her car, taken it for a joy ride, then ditched it." Even I couldn't imagine anyone wanting to joy ride in that decrepit vehicle, but you never knew. Kids could do dumb things.

"Not likely," Harold insisted. I had to agree.

"Maybe she pushed it into the river herself to claim the insurance," I suggested. "She could use a new car."

"She's a Rottman, not a Gold, Adam. Rottmans don't do such things. Besides, the comprehensive insurance would pay only the blue book value of that car, which is zilch."

I hoped against hope that if Sarah did go into the river she somehow escaped and was rescued and was now lying comatose in some LA hospital among the abandoned elderly and the indigent. "Has anyone checked the hospitals?"

"You can," Harold said. "I need you to go out there and look for her. Check on things. Talk to the police."

I dreaded making the rounds of Los Angeles hospitals. Losing my only sister was only part of the trauma. If Sarah didn't turn up alive by some miracle Harold was certain to ask me to take over the task of clearing out her godawful apartment. What to do with all those damned dolls and her clutter of junk? Schmuel might well drive up with a U-Haul truck and steal what Sarah always called in capital letters The Collection.

Harold misunderstood my hesitation. "Don't worry about the air fare, Adam. I'll pay all your expenses. You'll need to rent a car. For now just go out and find Sarah."

For now? What about later? What did Harold have in mind? Whatever it was he wasn't telling.

"Do you think this has anything to do with that tontine thing? That somebody might kill her?"

Harold was noncommittal. "Who knows?"

That tontine bugged me. "Was that inheritance thing all Sadie's idea?"

Harold was silent.

I continued. "I mean, I can't imagine anybody being so, so diabolical. It's a crazy thing to do."

Now Harold was defensive. "Sadie wasn't crazy. She was of sound mind and body."

"Hey, Harold, she was over ninety. The elderly make weird decisions. Why didn't you talk her out of it?"

"I didn't want to interfere."

"Maybe you should have," I said. "Maybe this wouldn't be happening. If one of the relatives killed her because of this..."

Harold got the point. "Don't try to lay a guilt trip on me, Adam. Just go out and find Sarah."

Deborah was not keen on my leaving again so soon. She gave out this shriek, "Whaaat! You just got back," but I suspected what she'd miss was my cooking. Deborah doesn't like to cook. She says she's a professional woman. Sometimes I think she didn't want a husband, but a maid. Before I retired we had a woman come in once a week. Now I'm chief cook and vacuum driver. I don't mind. Deborah says being a house spouse brings out my nurturing side.

I was afraid she'd buy her meals at a drive-through Mickey D's and eat in her Camry. "Just so you won't ruin that lovely figure on restaurant food, I'll lay on some Healthy Choice frozen dinners," I promised.

I would have preferred to make up a week's worth of home cooked dinners and freeze them myself. There wasn't time for me to make a gallon or two of twelve bean soup. Deborah loves my twelve bean soup but I knew she wouldn't want to thaw out a frozen portion dinner after dinner. Frozen dinners would have to do.

I was able to get a reservation to LA First Class, since Harold was paying. I couldn't help but feel a cold chill around my kidneys at the thought that Sarah's driving her VW into the Los Angeles river hadn't been an accident.

If Sarah was really dead, which I fervently prayed wasn't the case, Aunt Sadie's diabolical tontine would kick in. If Sarah's disappearance wasn't an accident, if someone had killed her, then I was on the list of possible victims.

6.

When Sarah had picked me up at LAX I had relied on her experience of the congested freeways to get us to North Hollywood without being shot at, forced off the road, or rear-ended. The rental car I picked up at the airport turned out to be a red Mitsubishi. I remembered the name from World War II. First they bombed us with their planes; now they're selling us their cars. No hard feelings. Business is business unless you're in the infantry. Then it doesn't matter much who manufactured the weapon that kills you. You're still dead and national loyalty doesn't help you any.

The map the car rental kid provided got me out of the airport and more or less in the right direction.

I wished I had rented one of those new fangled talking cars with a built in map and guide system that tells you to take the next exit and turn right. I had to rely on my own sense of direction, not so easy. At that time of year LA was overcast and I couldn't see the sun.

After getting lost and asking directions of three people before I found one who spoke English I finally arrived at Sarah's apartment. I didn't have a key, of course, but Harold had prepared the ground and the super was expecting someone to show up.

Sarah's apartment manager Mr. Svenson is an old guy in his seventies who, she had told me, is an impatient handyman who got tired of fixing her clogged garbage disposal and removed it entirely. I suspect that he took the job at his age because supers' jobs usually come with a rent free apartment and you can't live on Social Security. Svenson is a skinny man with a little round belly and red Home Depot suspenders to keep his carpenter's tool belt from dropping his faded jeans.

Svenson is a suspicious type, no doubt from having to work with tenants who are would-be film stars without work and might go back to Iowa without paying the rent. "You got some ID?" he insisted.

I showed him my Michigan driver's license. I apologized. "It's an old picture. I had a beard then. My wife made me shave it off."

He gave me a look like maybe I wasn't playing with a full deck. "I noticed."

When he handed me a set of keys Svenson said, "You're the second one to try to get into her apartment. Your brother was insistent that only you should have access, either you or the cops. They'd need a search warrant."

"Yeh," I said. "You never can tell about the LA cops. Some do a little burglary on the side. So who was the first one to try to get into Sarah's place?"

"Wouldn't give his name."

"What's he look like? Age? Height? Weight?" I asked, then thought of Schmuel and his threat to grab The Collection. "Sunglasses?"

"Might have been," Svenson said. He didn't elaborate.

I wouldn't want to be a police interrogator trying to squeeze a confession out of Mr. Svenson. I didn't have a rubber hose or cattle prod to induce him to say more. I had to be satisfied with a set of Sarah's keys. I'd stay in her apartment, as much investigator as guard dog in case Schmuel showed up with a rented truck.

It was creepy, letting myself into Sarah's apartment. According to the custom, the tall seven day Shiva candle for Aunt Sadie had not been put out when Sarah left her apartment. It was still flickering in its blue glass holder on the mantelpiece. It had been less than a week since I watched Sarah light it for Aunt Sadie, and now, for all I knew, Sarah was gone, too.

It wasn't easy to find a place to put down my suitcase. The floor was cluttered with files, bits of packing popcorn from doll shipments, and those Raggedy Ann and Andys all staring at me with their emotionless shoe button eyes. "Who are you? What are you doing in our space?" they seemed to ask. I stifled an impulse to tell them I was just visiting. If I started talking to dolls Deborah would have me on her consultation couch when I got back to Michigan. That is, providing my rental car wasn't also found in the LA river with me missing.

It took some searching to find the LA phone books, which turned up under the couch. I gave up looking for a place to move them so just sat on a pile of dolls while I called all the LA hospitals.

It was a long list. None had a patient named Sarah Rottman. I felt empty and was losing hope.

It took three calls before I found out where I might find Sarah's car. As soon as the water subsided, her Volkswagen had been fished out of the concrete ditch Angelinos call a river. It was in an impoundment lot at the edge of town. That might mean half way to Vegas.

I asked three times of an ever more impatient bureaucrat how to get to the impoundment lot from North Hollywood while I wrote down the directions. Some people don't know how to explain things. How was I to know where the old drug store had been before it burned down and which direction was "take a left" from there? It depended on where you were coming from in the first place. I resolved to buy an LA map as soon as possible, a real one.

When I stopped at a Shell station for a map there were a couple of Hispanics lurking around the place. Could they be car jackers? Just in case, I took the keys and locked the car before going inside the gas station.

It was easier with a map. I kept it spread on the steering wheel, glancing at it from time to time when I wasn't evading lane switchers. The police impoundment lot where I was told Sarah's car could be found was behind a high chain link fence with concertina wire on top. I guessed the fence was to keep irate owners whose cars had been towed from sneaking in to steal back their own vehicles.

The guard wore a mean expression and the dregs of what once must have been a uniform. The faded jacket didn't fit and wasn't buttoned. Though he looked too old to be of that generation, the guy wore a baseball cap with the bill in the back. Figuring me for an irate car owner, he immediately gave me a hassle.

I tried to be civil. No, I didn't want to fetch the car, which required that I fork over the retrieval and towing charges plus the daily fee. I just wanted to look at the car to make sure it was, in fact, Sarah's. Then I'd be back.

I had no intention of bailing out Sarah's dead car. What would I do with an elderly Volkswagen that had taken a swim and drowned in the LA river? This was one car the impoundment racketeers couldn't smuggle aboard a container bound for countries unknown, another of the scams used to fatten the income of the impoundment folks and their corrupt cohorts.

The impoundment lot was a sorry place, indeed. Amidst the obviously abandoned cars with their flat tires and load of grime there were new BMW's and other expensive cars that no doubt were destined for midnight export if their owners didn't show up and pay the extortion fees tootsweet.

Sarah's sad beetle was squeezed in between a battered Trans-am and a faded Buick that had once been maroon, a bad color for California. The cars were packed in so tightly that I couldn't slip between them. To see inside Sarah's VW I'd have to climb up on the muddy hood and wipe the silt off the windshield. I didn't want to get filthy or to smell like river bottom, but it had to be done. I wondered where Sarah dropped off her dry cleaning, if she ever did.

As carefully as I could to avoid rolling in old dreck I got up on the hood, wiped the windshield with my handkerchief, and looked inside. It was not happy sight.

I tried to remember the routine for escaping from a car that has gone off the end of a dock. You were supposed to wait until it filled up enough so you could open the door against the pressure of the water. Or you could take a breath of the air trapped inside, roll down the window, and swim out. I doubted if Sarah's stout hips would make it through a VW window. Escape is more difficult if the car turns upside down and it's dark.

The thought of sweet Sarah in her pigtails and Raggedy Ann apron frantically trying to escape from a car as it tumbled in the dark through the rushing waters of the Los Angeles river gave me a clutch of fear as if I might, too, end up in the same situation.

Kneeling on the hood I could see that the driver's side window was open or broken out. I couldn't tell which. Sarah might have gotten out that way. Of course, the door might have been open when they found the car. It was shut now.

I couldn't see into the back seat and briefly debated whether I wanted to crawl over the top and peek inside the rear window. I decided against it. There was mud all over the upholstery, an even coating of brown yuck where before there had been torn and faded plaid.

Something was missing. I couldn't place what it was. Puzzled, I eased off the hood with minimum dirt on my pants, brushed what I could off my knees, and returned to the impoundment office.

The surly guard's expression had been developed by countless encounters with irate, dead beat car owners. His pitch was well rehearsed from past repetition. "You gonna pay the bill? You can't have the car unless you pay the bill. Cash or certified check. We don't take credit cards or personal checks."

"Tell you what," I offered. "I'll make you a present of the car."

"Look, Mack, even if you give the car to the State of California, you still have to pay the bill."

I found myself unexpectedly overcome with grief. "Hey, guy. The car was fished out of the river. It belongs to my sister, who may be dead. If she doesn't show up alive, nobody's going to claim the car and they're not going to pay your goddam bill, either." Frustrated and ashamed, I could feel the tears coming. Funny how you can suppress grief most of the time and then it grabs you without warning at the most inconvenient moments.

"Too bad about your sister," he said without sincerity. "The county will put a lien on her estate."

"She has no assets," I said. "All she owns..." I kept it in the present tense, not wanting to admit that Sarah was probably dead... "is a bunch of Raggedy Ann dolls."

I turned away and managed to get back to the rental car before I broke down and sobbed. Poor Sarah. It was only after I got back in the car and tried to get my bearings for the drive back into the city that I remembered what was missing.

Sarah had had a little Raggedy Ann dangling from her rear view mirror. Had it come off during the car's tumble in the river? Had someone stolen it? Whatever the reason, it was gone.

7.

My calls to the hospitals had been fruitless. The LAPD weren't much help, either. They already had Sarah down in their book of missing persons, but in LA there are so many of them-- runaway kids, derelict husbands fleeing child support payments, and genuine mysterious disappearances-- that unless a body turns up in a dumpster they don't make much effort. The woman who took down my name and the phone number at Sarah's apartment was polite but not hopeful. "If she did get swept out in the ocean she might turn up on one of the beaches."

I was grateful the clerk avoided vivid details. She didn't go into lurid descriptions of corpses noshed on by sharks and crabs, then battered in the surf. I was sure that if Sarah turned up on the beach at Santa Monica it wouldn't be as a sun bather or as a street vendor hawking collectible dolls.

"How do you know she didn't go on an unexpected holiday, Mr. Rottman? She might be down in Tiajuana for a few days."

I wasn't hopeful. The first check from Aunt Sadie's trust wouldn't arrive for a couple of months. Sarah didn't have the money for bus fare. You couldn't buy a bus ticket to Mexico with food stamps. I couldn't see Sarah hitching to the border in her Raggedy Ann apron and pigtails. Someone would take her for an elderly hooker with a kinky fantasy. "That wouldn't explain how her car got into the river."

Stymied, I returned to Sarah's place. Her cluttered garage would have freaked out any inspecting fire marshal. There was barely room to open the driver's door to get out when I parked. The kitchen was worse than I remembered it. Though she had a double sink, the left side was stacked with washed dishes. I recognized the glasses she had used when she served up that Mogen David wine for Aunt Sadie's mourners. She hadn't put them away, probably because her cupboards were already overflowing.

The fridge door had a collection of Raggedy Ann and Andy magnets. I shook my head at the sight. How do you spell o-b-s-e-s-s-i-o-n? Inside, the few vegetables had wilted and faded-- some rubbery carrots, a tomato gone soft, something that might have been broccoli once. Sarah had a tub of vegetable dip with gray mold around the edges.

Besides collecting dolls Sarah had clipped grocery coupons and had a coffee can stuffed with them. Most were outdated. To make room on the counter I threw them all out and tried to put a dent in the kitchen mess. I found a trash bag and was busy filling it when the phone rang.

On the sixth ring I found the buried phone near Sarah's computer. "Hello?" Who knew I was there? Only Harold, I thought. It was late afternoon in L.A. and past brother Harold's bed time back east in Indianapolis. It wasn't him.

"Adam?"

"Yes. Who's this?"

"Millie. Harold said you'd be coming out to check on Sarah. Did you find out anything?" It sounded like she was afraid I might have.

She sounded so guilty that I wondered if Millie might be involved in Sarah's disappearance in some inexplicable way. Was she asking for herself, or was someone else using her to check on my progress? "I found the car in the impoundment lot," I said.

"Did you drive it back?"

I remembered that Millie didn't drive, knew nothing about cars. "I don't think anyone will be driving it again. Drowned cars are pretty useless once water gets in the engine and the electrical system, not to mention stinky river dreck in the carpets, headliner and upholstery. The cleaning job would be more expensive than the car's worth."

My explanation was wasted on her. She asked, "Did you go to the police?"

"Sure, but missing persons in LA are as common as shoplifters in K-Mart at Christmas."

"What will you do if she doesn't turn up?"

She was plainly asking for my plan of attack. "I don't know," I said, then, remembered Schmuel and guessed that he might be the impetus behind her call. I added for his benefit, "Harold advised me

31

to stay here and guard the place from any goniff who might want to steal the dolls."

"Oh," Millie said, faintly, like maybe that was what she had in mind herself. I couldn't imagine Millie stealing anything, but she's got the Gold chromosome.

Just to intimidate anyone else who might be with her I added, "I hear that in LA if you shoot a burglar he has to be inside your house and you can't shoot him in the back."

Millie's voice was fainter than ever. "You got a gun, Adam?"

Of course I didn't. "This is Los Angeles," I said. "Doesn't everybody?" Aunt Sadie didn't. She had her cane. If she had packed heat as they say in the hood, she'd have shot that Mercedes driver in the zebra crossing and pleaded self defense.

"How long are you going to stay in town?" Millie asked.

"I don't know. A few days."

"Would you like to come over for dinner?"

I remembered Deborah's caution about not eating anything served by the cousins. Or had Harold said that? I put her off. "Maybe later, after I get my bearings. We could 'do lunch' as you say out here."

"Denny's has a senior menu, very reasonable," Millie suggested.

"Don't worry, Millie. I'll take you anywhere you like."

"Denny's is fine," she said. Millie is modest. Maybe she got in the habit of picking out the cheapest thing on the menu from tight Aunt Sadie.

"Whatever you like. I'll take you to Denny's. Driving in LA is not like Michigan, but I got a street map. I might be able to find Fairfax Avenue. I'll get back to you." I was about to hang up when I remembered something that had puzzled me. "Did you call the police to report Sarah as a missing person?"

"No."

"Any idea who did?"

There was a pause at the other end. Looking back, I think that maybe she covered the mouthpiece while she asked someone else in the room. Her answer sounded too informed for someone who didn't drive. "Maybe the police found the car and her name on the registration. Then they'd try to reach her."

I couldn't imagine any document readable with all that river schmuts. Then I remembered the license plate. The police could get her address from that, but of course Sarah wasn't home. "And if they didn't? Who would they know to call?"

"Her landlord, I suppose," Millie suggested.

"I'll ask him," I said, made a mental note of the task, and hung up.

The conversation had been unnatural. Not that I've talked much to my cousin Millie on the phone, not ever, but I had the feeling that Millie had wanted to say something else to me and couldn't, either because she simply lacks conversational skills or someone else was with her and she was afraid. Afraid. That was it. Millie sounded like she was afraid of something, or someone.

8.

Staying the night at sister Sarah's was not exactly like dropping in at a motel or being an expected guest. I would have preferred a hotel, but Harold wanted me to keep an eye on Sarah's place just in case. That meant moving in.

I hadn't seen Sarah's bedroom before and was appalled. Her bed hadn't been made nor the sheets changed. I recognized the coverlet as one that had belonged to our mother of blessed memory. Raggedy Anns and a much hugged oversize teddy bear nearly filled the bed.

Sarah's discarded laundry was all over the bedroom floor and her closets were full. It looked like she shopped at the Goodwill then decided not to wear the stuff. Compulsive and sloppy. If she turned up alive, which I hoped, I would have to find a tactful way to induce her to clean up her mess. There was no place to put anything. Finally I pulled everything off the bed and searched for a clean sheet.

I did not want to sleep in my missing sister's bed, even if I did clear it off but there was no alternative. I felt put upon, frustrated, disgusted and angry. Surely Harold hadn't any idea of what he was asking when he insisted I stay there.

If I stayed very long I'd have to buy some food which meant finding the nearest grocery. I had to get away from that mess in the apartment to wipe visions of Sarah's dirty laundry out of my head. Was there a Laundromat somewhere? I locked the apartment door and parked the sack of kitchen trash outside Sarah's screen door with its burglar resistant steel grating-- a standard feature of homes in southern California.

There was no Laundromat. I found a little Korean ma and pa grocery a block away, had my choice of a Vietnamese or a Mexican restaurant, chose Vietnamese and ordered a number 72 which turned out to be a vegetarian platter. At the Korean place I picked up a loaf of bread and a jar of Guava jam for breakfast. I'd knew where Sarah kept her coffee and had discovered the toaster under a nearly empty box of shredded wheat.

Fortified with a meal, I returned to the apartment.

The bag of kitchen trash was not as I had left it. It had been right in front of the grated screen door. I hadn't locked that. Now the bag of trash was to one side. Someone had gone through it.

A raccoon or a dog would have left a mess behind. Whoever had inspected Sarah's leavings had made a hasty effort to put it back, but hadn't returned it to the spot where I left it.

Uneasy, I wondered if someone had gotten into the place. There are still people in Lansing who never lock their doors. This wasn't Lansing. I regretted not having locked the screen door. Had someone gotten in? Would I have any clue if something was missing?

I put down my sack of bread and jam and cautiously opened the apartment door. It was dark inside, lit faintly by Sadie's Shiva candle on the mantle. The candles are made to burn for seven days, and it had not yet been a week since Sarah lit it. I switched on the light.

In today's world of toys with computer chips and batteries I might have been greeted by a chorus of, "Hi, there. Want to play?" but the old fashioned Raggedies were silent. I imagined them to be accusing: "Why weren't you here to protect us?"

There was no one in the apartment. Whoever had checked out the trash would probably be back. I'd wait.

I wondered if Goldilocks had felt the same apprehension when she lay down in Mama Bear's bed. It was an invasion of her private space for me to sleep in Sarah's bed. Sarah did have a television and in my clearing off the bed linen I had stumbled on the remote control. I took off my shoes and settled in using the giant teddy bear for a pillow.

Outside, it started to rain. The screened porch at the back of Sarah's place had a corrugated fiberglass roof and the raindrops declared a shower, not a cloudburst or drizzle.

Half way through the Letterman show I heard a noise at the front door.

Trying not to fall over the junk in the living room, I crept in my stocking feet to the door and listened. Someone was trying various keys on the screen door lock. They couldn't get it open, so I was safe to open the inside door. I reached for the light switch and flung the door open in a quick movement to catch whoever it was by surprise. "Who's there?"

I didn't recognize him without his sunglasses.

"Don't shoot! It's me, Schmuel."

I didn't let him in. "What are you doing here?"

He tried to make up an excuse, but Schmuel the schlemiel isn't capable of smooth talk.

"You could have knocked," I said, still not opening the door.

"I didn't think you were here. Can I come in? It's raining."

"I'm not decent," I said, as if stocking feet wasn't proper attire for a cousin. "So what do you want?"

Instead of answering, he gave me another question. "How long are you staying?"

"Harold asked me to try to find Sarah. If she doesn't turn up I guess I'll have to see to her stuff."

"Need any help? I can help. I'm very helpful."

Schmuel looked like one of those helpers who never lifts a finger except to point and say, "Put it over there." "Was it you who went through her trash?"

"Me? Do I look like a dumpster diver?"

Answering a question with a question is a Yiddishism I nearly forgot, living in Wasp country. "Look, Schmuel, if I need any help, I'll call you. Your number is in Sarah's Rolodex."

"OK." Schmuel left.

I was glad it was Schmuel who had tried to get in and not a gang of East Los Angeles thugs wanting to lift Sarah's television and computer. What would I do, chase them in the dark in the rain in my stocking feet and yell, "Stop or I'll spit?" That wouldn't be respectful. I heard if you don't show proper respect you can get knifed.

I went back to Sarah's bed and the last of the Letterman show. I would call Harold in the morning for further instructions. I set Sarah's TV to "sleep" and sometime during the Late Late show I did.

9.

Another round of calls to the hospitals the next day produced nothing nor had the LA men in blue turned up Sarah, dead or alive. It was a mystery. I phoned Harold at his office in Indianapolis to report. His paralegal put me through.

Harold didn't seem surprised that I hadn't found Sarah. Maybe he just has no confidence in me as an amateur detective. All business, Harold said, "The collection is a valuable part of Sarah's estate. I'm arranging for Mayflower moving company to pick up her stuff. Everything."

"Even down to half a box of shredded wheat?" I asked. "Aren't you being hasty? We don't know for sure that she's dead."

"Moving the collection is for safe keeping," Harold explained.

"Where's it going? Into storage here in LA or what?"

"I can't risk the cousins getting their hands on Sarah's stuff," Harold said.

I knew he was protective of our little sister, but if she was actually dead, did it matter? The cousins couldn't inherit it. Unless she had a will stating something otherwise, like giving the dolls to a museum, Harold and I were her only heirs. The thought of us two brothers pouncing on poor Sarah's meager possessions made me queasy. "So where's it to be moved to? Do you want me to rent a storage locker here in LA?"

"No. It's going to our summer house."

What Harold was really saying was to his summer house. It's not ours anymore.

Years ago our folks built a cottage in Michiana Shores near Lake Michigan at the Indiana-Michigan line. When they moved to Arizona, which turned out to be their final resting place, they offered the cottage to the three of us. Sarah, of course, didn't have any money. Deborah and I had just bought our home in Lansing and were in hock to the limits of our means, so Harold in all his affluence bought the house promising to let us come and use it.

The cottage is a nice place a safe distance from the Lake Michigan beach which comes and goes according to the water level. In high water years storms sometimes dismantle those houses, so it pays to be on the land side of the road. It also helps with the insurance rates and reduces storm-induced insomnia.

The three of us used to spend our summers there, lying about in the sand, keeping an eye on little Sarah in her toddlerhood when she possessed only one Raggedy Ann. At this time of the year the place is all shut up.

"You're expecting to move all of Sarah's shit all the way to Michiana? Where will you store it? "

"In the garage," Harold explained. "There's plenty of room. You stay in LA until I can get the move arranged."

I was too shocked to speak up. At Sadie's wake even timid cousin Millie was bold enough to ask if Sadie had left any money. Inheritance was high on the minds of the Gold cousins. I didn't expect Harold, always quick to identify himself as a Rottman, to swoop down so suddenly and grab Sarah's stuff, which meant The Collection, and to put it in his--not our-- garage at the lake. Possession, my lawyer brother was always quick to say, is nine tenths of the law.

Not that I wanted any of those dolls. The one Sarah gave me when she drove me to the airport was more than enough. But the idea of grabbing Sarah's stuff when I couldn't be sure she was dead was a manifestation of greed I'd expect from a Gold, not a Rottman.

I suppose that having paid Sarah's rent all these years Harold could claim a lien on her personal property. I had to acquiesce. If Sarah wasn't coming back and the trust would no longer be obliged to pay her anything, there was no point in Harold paying the rent on the apartment. The movers would come, I could go home, and Mr. Svenson would take the clean up costs out of the damage deposit. I agreed to wait for the movers, but it left a bad taste in my mouth.

Calling the hospitals and the cops every day wasn't very demanding. I thought briefly about driving down to Santa Monica or wherever the LA river regurgitates old cars, skateboarders, and LA trash into the Pacific, and poke around looking for Sarah. It was not a happy thought.

What would I do in the meantime? I had no desire to see Schmuel. Cousin Jake was back in Chicago where he belonged. The only person I knew in LA was Millie.

I had promised to call and take her to Denny's for lunch. That would be one way to kill some time when I wasn't searching for Sarah. Maybe Millie would reveal even more about the perverse mind of our late Aunt Sadie.

10.

Cousin Millie was pleased to get my call. Her job at the Good Will store was only part time in the afternoons. As long as I could drop her off by two o'clock she'd be OK. I had her address in the Fairfax district and told her I'd pick her up and we'd drive to her favorite Denny's. I got out my LA map and tried to figure out the best way to get to her place without disappearing into some freeway fourth dimension.

Those interchanges come up fast. I got boxed into an exit-only lane by a truck full of migrant workers and found myself headed toward Santa Barbara, then had to find my way back. I was acquiring a healthy dislike for LA freeway traffic.

Eventually I made it to the Fairfax district. This was clearly a Jewish neighborhood. The word kosher in both English and Hebrew was featured on the windows of the delis, restaurants, and specialty food shops. I wondered if the neighborhood Denny's menu would be shrimp and pork free.

Surprise: people there walk. The sidewalks were crowded with shoppers and strollers. Among the pedestrians were occasional men in long, black caftans, wide-brimmed hats, earlocks and beards.

Funny how distinctive some LA neighborhoods can be. When I visited Sarah years ago she took me to Venice Beach, full of muscle men holding hands, skateboarders, and weirdoes. Santa Monica had its street vendors. Hollywood and Vine was paved with gawkers and hookers. Rodeo Drive was full of trophy wives driving Mercedes, Rolls Royces, and BMWs.

I couldn't find a parking place for my Mitsubishi rental, so I slowly cruised around the block and hoped to spot Millie in front of her place. On the third time around, there she was on the other side of the street wearing a shapeless flowered dress only the Good Will would stock.

I stopped in the traffic, rolled down the window and shouted to her. "Millie! I'll meet you at the corner over there."

Millie saw me. She was carrying an oversize purse, the kind that attracts the attention of store detectives wary of elderly shoplifters. Without looking, Millie stepped into the street.

I yelled to her, "At the crosswalk," but she didn't stop. She turned to check the oncoming traffic too late.

The scene fixed in my mind like one of those stop action sequences in the movies, frame by frame. A big, silver Mercedes struck her in the left hip. She went up in the air like a rag doll.

The purse flew, scattering its contents. One of the objects was a banana. I remember wondering, why is she carrying a banana in her purse? I keep seeing that freeze frame banana caught in mid flight.

There was a screech of brakes and the sound of women screaming. I nearly got hit myself, getting out of my car. Before I could work my way across the street a crowd had gathered around Millie. "Excuse me!" I said, pushing my way to the front. "That's my cousin. Please..."

Looking like an anachronism, an Orthodox Jew with beard, earlocks and black clothing had a cell phone and was calling 911. A middle aged woman in pink shorts, a halter top and a big hat picked up Millie's purse and was gathering her stuff off the pavement.

I tried to get closer to Millie. She was unconscious. There was blood coming out of her ears and nose. "I'm her cousin," I said to no one in particular.

The lady in the pink shorts handed me Millie's purse. Funny how these details stick with you. I was wondering what happened to the banana! Crazy.

The ambulance came in about two minutes, almost as if they'd been waiting in the wings for their cue. Two police cars showed up and the cops shooed everyone out of the way while the paramedics checked her out. They got out a gurney and gently lifted Millie onto it, careful not to move her head in case her neck was broken.

I stood on the street side of the Mercedes. Two cops questioned the distraught driver. One officer was Hispanic and looked barely got out of high school. The other was black, somewhat older. I tried to overhear what they were saying.

"I just got it out of the shop," the driver of the Mercedes explained, exasperated. He was dark skinned, looked like he might be one of those Iranian Jews who moved to LA when the Shah was kicked out. "A couple of months ago some crazy maniac woman dented the hood with her cane. Then she threatened to kill me. People here are nuts. That woman,"-- and here he pointed in the direction of the disappearing ambulance-- "stepped right out in front of me. She should get a ticket for jaywalking!"

Typical. He nearly kills a woman and wants the cops to give her a ticket.

I ran my hands over the hood of the Mercedes. It sounded like the one in the story Millie had told but I couldn't know what kind of a dent Aunt Sadie had put in the car. Was it the same car? If so, the body shop had done a good job. Striking Millie had put a dent above the grill. No doubt the Iranian's insurance company would be having second thoughts.

It was an odd coincidence. Millie had been with Sadie when she had nearly been hit in the crosswalk. Maybe the guy's Nazi car was prejudiced against little old Jewish ladies.

I hung around until the police finished taking down the driver's statement and wrote up the incident. Then I approached them. "Can you tell me what hospital they've taken her to? The victim is my cousin, Millie Gold. I was going to pick her up for lunch." I gestured to my car double parked across the street. "I told her to cross at the corner."

The Hispanic cop turned to me and seemed to be memorizing my face. "You've better move that car or it'll be towed."

I didn't want to encounter the surly gate guard at the impoundment lot a second time. "Right away. Just tell me what hospital they've taken her to."

The black officer intervened. "Probably Mount Sinai. So you can identify the victim?"

"Yes. My cousin, Millie Gold." I glanced nervously back at the Mitsubishi. I could imagine the tow truck coming any second.

"Got some ID?" the Hispanic officer asked. He had his notebook ready.

"I saw it happen," I said as I showed him my Michigan driver's license. "It was clearly Millie's fault. She didn't look." I shouldn't have said that.

The Iranian who had struck Millie caught my words. "You hear what he say? It was the lady's fault. She ran in front of me."

Oh, no, I thought. Millie was off to the hospital. What did they charge for those little excursions in ambulances in LA? Four hundred dollars? Six hundred? So far as I knew, Millie had no health insurance. She wasn't old enough, I thought, for Medicare. Hell, the poor thing might be dead or dying and we were arguing about whose fault it was. Did California have no fault?

The police let the Iranian driver leave and continued their interrogation of me. Before they were finished, sure enough, a tow truck appeared, ready to haul my car away.

"Hey!" I shouted.

Fortunately, the black cop waved the tow truck driver off. Up to then that was my first positive experience with the LA police. When I called their missing persons office I hadn't gotten much sympathy. In fact, they were clearly tired of my daily reminders. The clerk already recognized my voice.

I gave the police Sarah's address and phone number where I could be reached. Then it was my turn to ask questions. "Can I have the name and address of the driver? I'll have to talk to him about insurance."

At the mention of insurance the two policemen exchanged looks like maybe Millie and I were part of an insurance fraud scheme. I'd seen on TV how some people in Los Angeles will load up a car full of people, pull in front of an expensive vehicle on the freeway and then slam on the brakes so they'll be rear ended. Then they file a pile of insurance claims for whiplash and back ailments. Others made a business of stepping in front of cars, being knocked down, and then suing. Doesn't anyone have honest work any more?

"Obviously this is no scam," I assured the police. "You saw Millie when they picked her up. The driver's name and address, please."

The Hispanic condescended to tear out a page of his notebook with the driver's particulars and handed it over palm up like a bell hop with a room key, expecting a tip. I got directions to Mount Sinai and they let me go.

Crossing the street I slipped on something. Now I knew what happened to Millie's flying banana. Run over. Fairfax avenue is not a safe place if you are a banana or a jaywalking Jewish lady.

Back in my car I studied the cop's handwriting. It was the clumsy hand of someone who had just learned to write, but readable. The blast of a horn behind me sent me on the way to the hospital.

Sarah missing and now Millie hit by a car. It was as if Aunt Sadie had put a curse on the whole family.

11.

While Millie was in the ER I called Schmuel's. He wasn't home but his wife Sylvia was. Her voice was cold even before I identified myself. "What do you want? Schmuel told me you were rude to him the other night."

"I don't want to get into that," I said. "I'm calling from Mount Sinai hospital. Millie's been hit by a car."

I told her the story, explaining that it looked like a head injury. "I didn't know helmets were required to cross the street in LA." Black humor-- that's a Jewish trait. If you are about to be whacked by a Cossack say something funny like, "You call that a horse?" Maybe he'll miss.

"That's why sensible people drive," Sylvia said. "Except down in Jewtown. Those people don't have any seckel."

Shicksa Sylvia was trying to be cute, practicing her Yiddish vocabulary on me and mispronouncing the word for horse sense. For once I felt sorry for Schmuel. Even he didn't deserve to be married to a bitch like that.

"Look, Sylvia, no cracks, please. My sister Sarah's missing and now Millie may be dying in the ER."

"It didn't take you long, did it?" Sylvia accused. "Can't wait to get your hooks into the million bucks. What did you do, push your sister in the river and cousin Millie in front of a car?"

I nearly choked. "I was back in Michigan when her car was found. I didn't know anything until Harold called me."

"You Yids will do anything for money," Sylvia said, "even bump off your own sister. You better not come around here."

"You're accusing me of pushing Millie in front of a car? Are you crazy?"

She'd had enough. "I don't want to talk to you. Here's Schmuel's cell phone number. You got a pencil? Can you read and write?"

Bitch. I wrote down the cell phone number at the bottom of the page the cop had given me with the Iranian's address. If anyone was capable of murder, it was Sylvia Gold, not me. Whatever happened to Sarah and Millie was accidental, I told myself. That Iranian didn't just hang around waiting for Sarah or Millie to step into the street. How could he have known about the tontine while Aunt Sadie was still alive? He wasn't a relative. Had someone hired him?

Obviously I was thinking irrationally. I missed Deborah's psychologist's firm hand and sensible outlook. It had to be sheer paranoia to think that before Aunt Sadie died someone besides my close-mouthed brother Harold knew about the trust and the tontine. If they did, maybe Sadie's death was hastened.

I hadn't seen Sadie's death certificate. I assumed she died of old age. You don't die of being ninety-three. Probably her heart stared to fail, couldn't keep the kidneys going, or the lungs got congested and she couldn't clear them. There were lots of ways to die without being given a lethal dose by a nurse bent on mercy killing or someone with the Gold chromosome greedy for money.

Standing by the pay phone in the hospital corridor, I reached Schmuel with the last of my pocket change and told the story again of Millie's accident. I was careful and explicit about how I had told her to cross at the corner, not in the middle of the block, and that the driver might have been the same one who almost ran over Sadie. Some drivers are accident prone, aggressive, careless, and plain dangerous.

Sister Sarah had been none of those. She was simply incompetent.

Schmuel said he'd be right over.

I knew by his body language that the doctor who came out of the ER with blood on his coat had bad news. Massive head injuries. She never regained consciousness. Cousin Millie was dead.

Schmuel was too late.

I was distraught, irrational. First Sarah and now Millie. I had heard deaths came in threes. That had to be superstition. First Aunt Sadie, then apparently Sarah, now Millie. I couldn't be sure about Sarah. Until we had a body she was missing, not dead. But now Millie. Would there be more?

12.

I couldn't help it. I was distraught. Deborah always says I'm a worrier, that I always expect the worst which almost never happens. If my wildest suspicions and paranoia were true and Millie had been hit deliberately-- a crazy idea, I admit-- I had to sound out the driver of the death car. I admit that only the most Byzantine convoluted plotter would engage a total stranger to run someone down with a car, but maybe he wasn't a stranger. Maybe there was a connection to someone in the Gold family. How could I know?

The Hispanic policeman had written the name and address of the driver of the Mercedes but no telephone number. There were no phone books at the pay telephone in the hospital corridor but the admitting clerk let me look at hers. Fortunately, it was not a common name for Los Angeles, like Smith, Brown, or Rodrigez. How many Yahya Raganis could there be?

The phone was answered by a woman whose accent was vaguely British. Perhaps she had learned British English taught by an adventurous English woman in an Iranian school like in The King and I.

So how do you pronounce Yahya? "Can I speak with Ya-hee-ah please?"

"Yahya" -- she pronounced it like yah-yah-- "is at the store," she said, and gave me the number.

It figured: he was in the carpet business. Lucky for him the embargo against Iranian imports had been lifted.

Yahya Ragani was with a customer but would be with me shortly. It gave me time to think how I might handle this. How do you tell a man he's just killed someone? How could I do it without sounding like I was going to blackmail him or squeeze him for insurance? This was delicate. I wished Deborah were with me. She'd know. Deborah is tactful to a fault.

"Yes? This is Mr. Ragani."

I took a deep breath. "I was a witness at your accident on Fairfax today. I saw the woman run in front of your car. The accident was entirely her fault," I said, hitting on a tactic. "If you need me as a witness, in case the police give you a bad time, I'd be glad to be of service."

That got him receptive. "Who is this speaking?"

"Adam Rottman." I gave him Sarah's address. "I'm only in LA for a few days on family business. The woman who ran in front of your car is my cousin, Millie Gold. Is that name familiar to you?"

"No." I detected a hint of suspicion in Mr. Ragani's voice. He didn't sound certain. "How is she? Are her injuries severe?"

"I'm afraid she's dead. The doctors here at Mount Sinai just told me."

"Oh, my god, that's terrible," Ragani said.

I don't know California law, but I do know that in Michigan a friend of mine who was in an accident with a fatality was automatically charged with a felony: involuntary manslaughter. Lucky he got two years probation, not two years in prison. I didn't want to suggest that to Mr. Ragani, not yet, but if he were unfamiliar with California law I might use it as leverage if he didn't cooperate.

"Are you sure the name Gold isn't familiar? Would you by any chance have any customers named Gold?"

Ragani thought a minute. "I sold a carpet to a Mrs. Gold in Beverly Hills."

"Would that be Mrs. Schmuel Gold? First name Sylvia?"

"I can't be certain. I'd have to look it up. This is very upsetting, Mr. Rottman. I am very, very sorry that your cousin has died. Perhaps when you arrange the funeral I can send flowers, a token of respect for your family. It's the least I can do."

"Thank you, Mr. Ragani, but no flowers. We're Jewish. We believe flowers are for the living."

"Then I will say kaddish for your cousin," Mr. Ragani said.

So, I had guessed right. He was Jewish. But I had not guessed that the same man who ran down cousin Millie and had an encounter with Aunt Sadie before she died had also sold a carpet to Schmuel and Sylvia Gold. It is a small world, after all.

Rug merchant is an ancient profession, I thought as I hung up the phone. The reputation is not much different than carpet bagger in the south. Smooth talking, but not entirely honest, and likely to sell you a bill of goods. I wondered if Schmuel and Sylvia Gold had any dealings with Yahya Ragani other than carpets.

13.

Harold had worked fast. The Mayflower movers came the same day as Millie's funeral. I tried to prepare the way for them by throwing out the obvious trash. I didn't want Sarah's accumulation of souvenir wine bottles and corks to be schlepped all the way to Indiana, even if Harold was paying the bill. It was hard to separate useless paper from what might be important.

The Mayflower moving team, three burly men capable of carrying a grand piano apiece, didn't care. At $3 apiece, they had plenty of cardboard boxes and carefully packed every one of those Raggedy Ann and Andy dolls, Sarah's dirty laundry, and would have taken my suitcase and shaving kit if I hadn't stopped them.

There were still some things in Sarah's freezer. I remembered what happened when I moved out of my apartment in college. I left my next door friends the keys so they could empty the fridge, but the building owner beat them to it. When they got there the frozen pizzas I had promised the neighbors were gone. Everyone had their fiddle-- the car impoundment people exporting abandoned vehicles to foreign destinations. In Israel they call it dredeling after the four sided Hanukah top: each got his own spin.

Mr. Svenson was waiting for his, watching from a distance. Maybe he was afraid the movers would take the kitchen appliances and the bathroom commode. Though he was only the super and not the owner of the building, he hung around like a vulture waiting for morsels. Mr. Svenson no doubt cleaned out refrigerators when tenants left in a hurry. He could sell their abandoned pots and pans at the Sunday flea market.

The Shiva candle for Aunt Sadie was down to its last inch. A mover asked if I wanted to pack it, too. "Leave it," I said. "It's for mourning. It's bad luck to blow it out." I was beginning to think the candle was bad luck for all of us, first Sarah and now Millie.

It might burn for another day. If Svenson took it it was on his head.

The Mayflower man backed away from the candle like it was some voodoo curse.

I had to leave the movers to their task while I found my way to Millie's funeral. Technically Jews are supposed to be buried within twenty-four hours. Embalming is against our religion. I had wondered who would make the arrangements for Millie's burial, since she was so poor. It turned out that Millie had paid her funeral expenses in advance when her husband died so they'd have adjacent plots at Mount Sinai cemetery.

Mount Sinai is next door to Forest Lawn where many movie celebrities are buried. It's acres and acres of graves on a slope overlooking a freeway, not a bad view if you're among the living, but the freeway noise never stops. From a distance you might not guess Mount Sinai is a cemetery. It's not like Forest Lawn with its gaudy memorials, mausoleums, and commemorative statues. All the Mount Sinai graves are flush with the ground for easy mowing and the markers are a uniform size in bronze.

I got to the cemetery early enough to revisit Aunt Sadie's plot. Aunt Sadie's marker wasn't in yet, just a small metal sign. You could still see where the sod had been put back in place on the new grave. The dedications of the grave markers take place on the first anniversary of the death.

I looked around for a stone to leave as a token. It's a Jewish custom to leave a stone at the grave. The cemetery management frowns on that because the lawn mowers can nick the blades on them or turn the stones into dangerous projectiles.

I stood over Sadie's grave and spoke to her. "Aunt Sadie, what have you done? A tontine? Was that some kind of joke? It's not a lottery. In a lottery you don't wait for all the losers to die." She didn't answer.

I located the chapel and was surprised that Cousin Arthur Gold from Calumet City, Indiana and his sister Miriam, the butcher's wife, both came to Millie's funeral. I hadn't seen them in years.

A special section for immediate family mourners was up on the stage behind a scrim curtain so if any of us got hysterical we'd have a modicum of privacy.

Harley L. Sachs

Harold wouldn't come. I guessed he didn't do funerals. He had not come to Sadie's even though he was her trustee and he didn't make the trip for Millie, either. Schmuel and his bitchy wife Sylvia were missing. I would have been alone in the space reserved for immediate family except for Arthur Gold and his sister Miriam. They flew in together from Chicago. That was a surprise.

Arthur Gold had put on weight. He wore an electric blue sport coat that looked like he'd bought it on Maxwell Street in Chicago. Maxwell Street is full of schlock shops with pullers out on the sidewalk to induce you to come inside and buy. "Hi, Adam," Arthur said, shaking my hand with his right while he adjusted the Mount Sinai yarmulke with his left. "It's been a long time."

Why would Arthur and his sister Miriam both drop everything for Millie's funeral if they hadn't come for Aunt Sadie's? I asked them. Arthur started to answer but his sister beat him to it. "Harold called us."

Dear brother Harold. I wouldn't think with his busy law practice he'd have time to tickle the family grapevine. There had to be more motivation. Even with a discounted compassionate fare, a flight to LA was expensive.

Arthur explained. "We got some legal papers from Harold's office about Sadie's trust. There's a rumor that the estate's worth one million."

He waited for me to confirm that. I didn't, so he continued, "Harold says Sarah is missing. Any sign of her?"

"Sylvia thinks Sarah ran away," I said. "Maybe she's hiding in Mexico for her health. I hope she is." I told them about the car fished out of the Los Angeles river.

"Then she is dead," Miriam said. "Too bad. I heard she collected stuff, like salt and pepper shakers or something."

"Dolls," I said. "Raggedy Ann and Andy."

Miriam shook her head. "It takes all kinds." Of which she was not one.

I wasn't sorry Jake didn't come to Millie's funeral. He always gives me the creeps with his flagrant air of criminality.

Millie's coffin was entirely of wood, according to custom. A solemn Mount Sinai employee led us to the open coffin so we could see that it was indeed Millie inside. In some parts of the country there have been scandals of the wrong people being buried. Mount Sinai was taking no chances of a lawsuit.

It was Millie, all right, in spite of the morticians' makeup to cover the injuries to her face.

Side by side, we gathered around the open coffin. Millie looked like she was sleeping. When we confirmed the identification of the deceased the attendant closed the lid. In a moment of panic I thought, "She'll suffocate in there," but of course she was already dead.

Up close, Arthur smelled of cigarette smoke. I remembered he ran a dive in Calumet City. "How's business?"

Arthur grinned with a shrug. "You know how it is. If the Indiana cops stage a raid, we run across the street to Illinois. If the Illinois cops raid, my competitors run over to our side. As long as the cops don't get together, we're OK."

I'd never been to Arthur's club, as he calls it. Harold had. He told me it's one of those joints where the girls hustle the patrons for watered down drinks and take their turns dancing nude on the bar. The smoking laws aren't enforced. As for prostitution, the story for the cops is if the girls want to date someone on their own it's their business, not the club owner's.

I wondered why my brother Harold would drop in at cousin Arthur's Cal City dive. Maybe he has clients there. People in Cal City need the assistance of a lot of lawyers to keep them out of what the cons call "the joint." Being a lawyer brings you in contact with a variety of people, not all of them old Jewish widows with strange ideas about inheritance.

Miriam is quite different from her brother Arthur. So far as I knew, her husband, whom she described as a meat cutter, not a butcher, is legitimate. They have a son, Ira, and a daughter. The daughter's married, but the son is still in college. When she was young Miriam didn't like the look of her eyebrows and plucked them out. She has to draw new ones on every day with a pencil. She wears no other makeup and keeps her black hair pulled back. Maybe her unattractiveness is deliberate.

"How are you these days, Miriam?" I asked in the hushed tones appropriate for a funeral chapel.

"I got a new job," she said and gave me a challenging look. "I drive a cab."

"A cab?" I asked, incredulous. "Isn't that dangerous?"

51

"We all take risks," Miriam said with a shrug. "Look at poor Millie. Killed crossing a street. Your wife's profession isn't so safe. I heard she's a psychiatrist who treats nut cases."

"Psychologist," I corrected, but caught the class envy. Cab drivers have little in common with psychologists. Maybe bartenders do.

So there we were, only three of us, sitting behind a thin curtain in the chapel at Mount Sinai to say good-bye to Millie. Schmuel and Sylvia hadn't appeared. We were an unlikely collection, bound by the terms of Aunt Sadie's perverse intention. I was thinking about that when the hired rabbi started the prayers.

A surprising number of Millie's friends had gathered in the cavernous chapel for the funeral. The whole staff of the Good Will showed up, as did many others, none of whom I knew. Millie might have been broke, but she made friends with a lot of people who cared enough about her to see her off. Now that she was dead I realized that Millie had exuded a warmth and friendliness that attracted people, not like the rest of the Gold cousins.

When we came to the kaddish memorial prayer for the dead, we all stood up. We made a feeble attempt at singing Odon Olom, Lord of the World, but few among the mourners, most of whom were gentile, knew the tune. Knowing the right tune for Odon Olom-- Lord of the World-- is difficult even for Jews, as the hymn has many traditional melodies.

When we got up to follow the hearse to the grave site the attendant, who recognized me from Sadie's funeral less than a week before, handed me a Shiva candle. I guess he figured I was chief mourner. I made a lame remark about not making a habit of this. I'd light it when I got home and hoped there wouldn't be any more corpses before this one burned out. Then we all proceeded to the grave site.

That's when Schmuel and Sylvia arrived. Caught in freeway traffic, Schmuel explained. Sylvia made a cutting remark about his driving ability. I hoped I would get a chance to grill them later about their choice in rug merchants.

There's something awesome and final when it comes your turn to toss in the spade full of dirt. The sound of the soil striking the wooden coffin is a reminder that one day it will be your turn down there in the hole.

Before they could escape, I collared Schmuel and Sylvia. "Did you know that the man who's car ran into Millie is the same one who sold you a Persian carpet?"

"What?" Schmuel hadn't a clue about that. "Nobody told me anything about the driver of the car."

Sylvia wasn't talking. I tried another approach. "In Michigan when you kill someone in a car accident, even if it's not your fault, it's an automatic two year felony, involuntary manslaughter. What do you know about this Yahya Rogani?"

"He's a crook," Sylvia said, but unlike her usual self, she didn't elaborate.

If I came out and asked if she hired Rogani to run down our cousin with his Mercedes I would look incredibly neurotic and stupid. The accident was just that, wasn't it? If it wasn't an accident and she had arranged it, asking her right out would be risky, so I shut up.

14.

When I got back to Sarah's apartment it was empty and the Mayflower crew were about to leave. As I was signing their papers the driver said, "There was some guy looking for you. I told him you'd gone to a funeral."

"Oh? What did he look like?"

"About your size. He was with a woman, good looking. Drove a Lexus."

The weather was cloudy. We were lucky it hadn't rained at the grave site. I looked up at the sky and remembered. "Did he wear sunglasses?"

"Yeh, he did."

A Lexus, sunglasses. "I think I know who it was." So that's why Schmuel missed the chapel service. He'd made a detour to check on Sarah's place. "Did the woman insult you?"

The driver took a handkerchief from the back pocket of his coveralls and wiped his forehead. "Not me. She said we should wash the truck, that it gave Mayflower movers a bad name."

"That's Sylvia, all right. My cousin's wife."

The driver's expression said better you than me. They drove off. Sarah's stuff was not a full load. They had another pickup to make before the truck took Sarah's Collection cross country to the cottage in Michiana Shores.

Sarah's place looked larger with all the dolls gone. All that remained on the floor were bits of packing materials she had never cleared up and a couple of unassembled packing boxes the movers had left behind. Gray squares of dust marked where the furniture had stood and never been moved for cleaning.

The movers had been considerate enough to leave my suitcase and shaving kit behind. The bed, TV, and all that dirty laundry were gone. They hadn't touched the flickering Shiva candle for Aunt Sadie. In the kitchen I saw that the toaster, coffee maker, and dishes were gone. They had forgotten to take the collection of Raggedy

Ann refrigerator magnets. I don't know why, but I gathered them up and put them in my suitcase.

There were a few things left in the freezer. As long as I was still present, Mr. Svenson hadn't removed Sarah's dregs from the fridge. The last of my loaf of bread and jam was still there.

I fervently hoped that dear brother Harold didn't expect me to clean the place before I left. It would take hours to clean that stove. I was afraid to look inside the oven.

This was not my turf. It was time for me to find a hotel or return to Michigan. I hadn't located Sarah and my prospects were nil. Maybe I should have Sarah's face and particulars printed on milk cartons like they do with missing children. If the LA police found Sarah's body, I'd return.

With all the furniture gone it was easy to find the phone. Harold's office was closed, and he wasn't at home. I left a message on his machine. "This is Adam. I just got back from Millie's funeral. The movers have left. I'm taking the next available flight back to Lansing. I haven't found Sarah." I didn't mention my suspicions about Yahya the rug merchant. That story was too long and I didn't want it sitting on a tape in Harold's machine. So much for that.

I left the candle.

When I handed over the spare set of keys I told Mr. Svenson, "There's some Guava jam in the fridge. Help yourself."

"What about your sister?" Mr. Svenson asked. "The rent's paid to the end of the month."

"No sign of her. I guess she's dead. If she's not she'll be awfully surprised to come back and find the place empty."

Mr. Svenson, for all his cynicism, was genuinely interested. He hitched up his heavy utility belt with its load of tools and hammer. "What's your next step?

I sensed that Svenson liked a good story, so I explained Sadie's tontine. "My Cousin Schmuel's wife had the audacity of accusing me of pushing Millie in front of a car. I'm going back to Michigan before she tries the same thing with me."

Svenson thought that pretty funny. "You are some family!" He said it like we were an exotic species suitable for the San Diego zoo.

I didn't laugh.

15.

I dropped the Mitsubishi at the rental lot, and took the shuttle to the LAX terminal. The best connection I could make was the red eye for Chicago, a late evening departure calling for a fitful few hours while we passed from Pacific to Central time. Then a plane load of zombies would stagger off, me in search of my connection for Michigan. I had to schlep my carry on about a mile to the LAX gate. Lucky my bag has wheels. You could get a heart attack trying to run from one gate to the other end of the airport to catch a plane. Surprise: cousins Arthur and Miriam were on the same flight.

They were not surprised to see me. "Keeping tabs on us, Adam?" Miriam asked.

Are all cab drivers so cynical and suspicious? Maybe it goes with the job. "Why would I do that?"

Arthur put down the USA Today he'd been reading. "Your brother sent us some legal documents. He explained the tontine. We're on the list of potential inheritors. The papers Harold sent don't specify the value of the estate, but Schmuel heard it's one million bucks."

"So? Are you in a hurry to collect? Only the last survivor gets it. You might have to live to be ninety."

Arthur had taken off his electric blue jacket and funeral tie. "A million bucks is a lot of money."

Money. Always money. "The tontine doesn't come into play as long as Sarah is alive."

"It looks like she's dead," Miriam said. "What if her body doesn't turn up?"

"I suppose there's some procedure in California to declare someone legally dead. If someone goes down in the ocean in a plane crash and no body is recovered you have to assume the person dead."

Arthur squirmed in his seat. "Don't talk about plane crashes when we're about to fly."

Miriam scoffed. "Hey, if you go down in a plane you'll be dead so quick you won't feel a thing."

"It's the time it takes to go down that gets me," Arthur said. "Then you get pulverized, smashed to smithereens."

I changed the subject. "Sarah could have survived the trip into the LA river in her Volkswagen. At least that's what I'm hoping. I don't expect to inherit anything from Aunt Sadie. I'm not interested in her money."

"Oh?" Miriam didn't believe me. Her eyes narrowed. Her forehead with the pencilled in eyebrows looked odd. "Schmuel says you shipped off her doll collection. I hear it's pretty valuable. Maybe a couple of hundred thousand."

Rumors. This family feeds on rumors and hearsay. "Their value is in the eye of the beholder," I said. "To me they're just a bunch of silly old dolls. Harold's afraid Schmuel would grab them. He's going to store her stuff up at the lake until she turns up, dead or alive."

"The lake?"

"The old summer cottage at Michiana Shores."

I realized immediately I shouldn't have said that. Nobody needed to know where the dolls were stored. They might be in the locked garage, but no one was there to keep an eye on things.

Miriam shook her head. "Dolls!" She and her meat cutter husband struggled for an existence. The idea of having a collection of dolls, for God's sake, worth thousands of dollars was to them beyond belief.

"That's her schtick," I said. "People will collect anything."

Miriam got up to go to the bathroom. "Watch my bag, Arthur." The airport police are wary of terrorists stuffing bombs in unattended bags, or leaving bombs in suitcases.

I took advantage of her absence. "Why did Miriam decide to be a cab driver? Isn't it dangerous, especially if you're a woman?"

Arthur gave me a pitying look. "What kind of a life is it if you don't take risks? You never take risks, do you Adam?"

"Me? I'm just a house spouse. My biggest risk is if I put bleach in the colored laundry." Danger is not my bag. I don't even ride roller coasters.

Arthur snorted derisively. "You wouldn't have the guts to drive a cab in Chicago."

"Why does Miriam? Is it some kind of machismo thing? Woman's lib or something?"

Arthur explained. "I talked her into it. There's what you call perks."

"Perks?" The only cabby's perk I could think of was an injured back lifting suitcases into the trunk.

Arthur showed his business card from his club. "We have some special cards, 'free drink with this card' and I give them out to the cab drivers. If someone in town is looking for a good time, the cabby gives them one of these. I put the driver's number on the back and when someone turns in the card for a drink, the cabby gets a little bonus. In a month it adds up."

I could see the possibilities. "Do cat houses to the same thing?"

Arthur smiled. "You're catching on. Only they call themselves escort services or massage therapists. Then there's always the drunks who are too smashed to count their change. Or people leave cameras and valuables behind. There's lots of ways a cab driver can make a little extra on the side."

"And no tax," I said.

Arthur scoffed, "Tax!" as if only a chump would pay income tax.

Miriam returned from the bathroom. I hadn't visualized her as a hustler, too, but I saw it ran in the family. It was just as well my cousins didn't live close by. If they weren't family I wouldn't associate with them at all.

I was in first class and Arthur and Miriam were in coach. After this conversation I was glad I wouldn't be seated near them. Guilt by association. As we stood in line to hand over our boarding passes Arthur turned to me. "You and your dear brother Harold think you've got this by the tail, don't you? Setting up that trust fund for Sadie, then grabbing Sarah's doll collection for yourselves. Harold's a smart ass. You better watch your back, Adam. Some people don't take kindly to schemes like that."

I protested. "Don't take this out on me. It's Sadie's doing." Imagine having a dead person jerk your chain.

They called for first class passengers to board. Thanks to Harold's paying the freight, that meant me. As I looked back over my shoulder at Arthur and his sister I caught his sudden change of expression. A moment before he had been friendly, giving me insider's tips on how to make money on the side. Now there was hatred in his eyes. That spooked me. One minute he was affable, now.... What had set him off? Was he envious because I was flying first class, and he and Miriam were in coach? It made me glad we were all on the same plane. Neither Arthur nor Miriam would bring down a plane to get me if they were both on the same flight.

It occurred to me that if someone else put a bomb on it we would all die. If Schmuel or Jake bombed the plane, eliminating three competitors for Sadie's money at one time would be a real shortcut to a fortune.

I could hardly wait to get back to my therapist. Good thing I married her. Saves those expensive consultation fees. Deborah would bring me out of this paranoia-- I hoped.

16.

It was a full plane, people taking advantage of the red eye price break, eager beaver businessmen giving up a decent night's rest so as not to miss a full day of trading. Even though I was in first class, the flight attendants pushed orange juice, coffee, and a bagel on the passengers just before the plane made its approach to O'Hare, then came by to snatch the paper cup out of my hand before I finished mine. Talk about rude. The quality of air travel-- yech!

The bagel reminded me of the one Sarah had pressed upon me before that other flight home. I was being haunted by bagels and cream cheese. I stubbornly kept the remaining half a bagel, wrapped it in my paper napkin, put it in my pocket, and stumbled off the plane, still angry at the fight attendant.

Cousins Arthur and Miriam got off after I did but I waited at the gate to say good-bye. One look at Arthur's face and I checked my own chin for stubble. Arthur's electric blue jacket was rumpled and he needed a shave. At least my eyebrows were still there. Miriam's weren't. The lines had smudged during the night and gave her an odd look between sleepy and surprised.

"Keep in touch," Arthur said. Either he was too tired to be angry or had mellowed during the flight. "In case anything comes up in this family business. You got my address?" He took out his wallet and produced a business card. "You can usually get me at the club. If you're ever in Calumet City drop by for a drink."

Remembering old stories I said, "I heard Cal City is a pretty rough place."

Arthur shrugged. "Maybe on Saturday nights. The bartenders always have a baseball bat handy if someone gets rambunctious. Sometimes my bouncer wears a bulletbpoof vest."

I hoped Arthur was kidding. His was not my sort of night spot. I looked at the business card before putting it in my shirt pocket. The blue ink matched Arthur's jacket. The name of the club was The Gents'. It was supposed to sound genteel and respectable, but the name reminded me of a toilet. How could he be so dumb? It would have been better to call it "The Office" or "The Library" for those calls to the wife at home, "I'm at the office. I'm working late," while some B girl strips on the bar and shakes her tits in your face.

Then again, maybe Arthur's "Gents'" was a toilet. I imagined putting a bar close to the urinals to shorten the trip between beer and piss.

When would I be in Calumet City? Turned out I would, sooner than I thought.

It was the last time I saw either Arthur or Miriam alive.

17.

Two trips across the country in a week. I was putting on significant frequent flyer miles. At this rate I'd soon qualify for a free round trip ticket to the moon. I hoped not to have to make any more trips to LA. I hoped that Sarah would turn up, bright and chipper in her Raggedy Ann braids and apron, and announce that she'd won a trip to Acapulco.

I hoped that my last relative in LA, Schmuel, would live a long and fruitless life and not step in front of any Mercedes driven by a crooked Iranian rug peddler.

When Deborah saw my face at our front door her welcoming smile turned to worry. "You look like hell."

"That's no way to greet your loving husband."

"What about this?" She gave me a hug and a kiss that promised more.

"That's better." I carried my suitcase into the laundry room and, dutiful house spouse, sorted my laundry into the appropriate hamper. While I was at it, I stripped, hung my slacks over one arm, took the now nearly empty suitcase in the other hand and walked to the bedroom.

Deborah's kiss had given me a hard on. She laughed when she saw me. "Showing off?"

"Why not?"

I put down the suitcase while I hung up the slacks. The luggage zipper wasn't closed and the Shiva candle for Millie rolled out.

"What's that?" Deborah asked. "Did you bring me something from California?"

"Sorry. No gift. It's a Shiva candle for Millie. Looks like I'm designated chief mourner. I'll light it later."

"What about Sarah?"

"No sign of her," I admitted. "I'm praying that she's not dead. I don't think I could handle another funeral." I thought of sweet, simple Sarah stuck in her child's obsession with dolls, half buried in LA river mud and gnawed by rats. My sister!

I started to cry. Except for that episode at the impoundment lot I had managed to bottle it up, but home with my wife there was no need to put up a show of bravado or mental toughness. I was coming apart from the stress.

Deborah, always the skilled psychologist, comforted me with an embrace that brought back my inspiration. I soon succumbed to her therapy. It was good to be home.

Deborah had canceled a couple of morning appointments so she could welcome me back, but she had to hurry to her office.

Alone in the house, I put Millie's mourning candle up on a saucer on the sideboard in the dining room. I didn't know the appropriate Hebrew prayer, so I improvised in English, "Praised be the Lord our God, Ruler of the universe, who commands us to light a candle in memory of the dead." I stopped short of covering mirrors and darkening all the rooms. The Rottmans aren't into Orthodox mourning.

I was back to the laundry, picking up the professional journals and copies of Cosmopolitan that Deborah left scattered on the coffee table. I'd need to do a refrigerator inventory, plan meals, make a grocery list and run the vacuum. With the vacuum cleaner doing its thing I didn't hear the ring, but when the message machine kicked in and I heard a voice, dropped the dust sucker and grabbed the phone. "Yes?"

It was brother Harold calling from Indianapolis. "How'd it go?"

"You know how it went," I said, testily. He was generous enough to foot the plane fare and car rental, but I was the one who had to represent the Rottmans and languish on the red eye. "I didn't find Sarah. That was what I went for. Maybe you should hire a real detective."

"Let's wait on that one. I know you didn't find Sarah. I meant Millie's funeral."

"On a scale of one to ten it was about a four," I said. "Schmuel was more interested in seeing if the movers were getting first dibs on the doll collection than in making it to Mount Sinai on time. But he did show up for kaddish at the grave."

"Good." Harold had trouble catching his breath. With all that weight he has emphysema, a perfect combination for a heart attack.

Something else was bothering him. "Jake and Schmuel asked a lawyer about the validity of Sadie's trust agreement."

"They want to break the will?"

"There was no will," Harold corrected. "It's an irrevocable trust."

My back was starting to hurt from all the bending. I sat down on Deborah's favorite chair, an overstuffed job in soft tan leather that she picked up for eight hundred dollars, and that was a sale. "Can they do that?"

"They can try," Harold wheezed, "but it won't do them any good."

"If Sarah's dead, then this tontine thing kicks in."

"They have to get a California court order presuming her death. I don't know if California is a common law state. I have to look it up."

"What's a common law state?" I wondered. "The only common law I ever heard of is common law marriage, like if you check into a motel in New York as Mr. and Mrs. you are legally married. Stuff like that."

Harold shifted into his lawyer mode. He spoke in double spaced formality. "Under common law, if there's a presumption of death, but no body, you have to wait seven years to collect on things like life insurance."

"And inheritance?"

"And inheritance," Harold confirmed.

"Then if our rapacious relatives decided to kill each other off-- and us-- if California is a common law state they have seven years before they can collect."

"If someone kills someone for an inheritance they can't collect," Harold reminded me.

"I guess they'll have to be more clever about it." I wondered if Michigan was a common law state. Old Mr. Kripe hadn't covered that in my high school social studies class a million years ago. If he had I was too busy contemplating Toots Trevor's tits to notice. Oh, those adolescent urges!

"You still there?" Harold asked.

"I was just thinking of Toots Trevor's tits," I said.

"Who's that?"

"Never mind. So if California isn't a common law state, Schmuel can ask that a death certificate be issued for Sarah. Then the heat's on. But if it is a common law state, if someone wants to hurry the tontine-- like maybe Jake putting a hit on all of us-- he has to wait seven years to collect?"

"It doesn't matter," Harold said. "Indiana is a common law state. The trust is here. Sarah has seven years to show up."

I hoped Sarah really was in Acapulco. "What would she live on? She hasn't any money."

"I'll keep an eye on her bank account," Harold said.

"How can you do that?"

"It's joint. Since I'm making the deposits from the trust, I'm a co-signer."

A co-signer, I thought. With rights of survivorship. Now my Gold chromosome came into action, turning on the suspicion. Harold had already grabbed the doll collection and all of Sarah's stuff. If he could take the trust deposits out of Sarah's accumulating bank account, did he also have his eyes on the alleged million dollars?

I knew some of Harold's clients were dead beats who never paid their fees. Those who got convicted couldn't. It takes a long time to pay back $200 an hour legal fees if you're in the state pen making license plates at twenty cents an hour. If the lawyer business was bad, four mil would make a nice retirement nest egg.

"Oh," was all I said, and let it hang. Let him think about my thinking about it.

Harold was about to ring off when I stopped him. "So if by any chance any of our precious cousins decides to bump the others off, it has to appear to be an accident, so they can't be accused and lose rights to inherit. Right?"

"Schmuel may have gone to a lawyer, but I don't think he's clever enough to get away with murder," Harold said. "Arthur may have some shady friends with homicidal tendencies. I don't know about Miriam."

I remembered my gangster cousin. He was prime suspect. "How about Jake? Jake could." But Jake could not have arranged Millie's death. He had no connection to Iranian rug merchants who drove through zebra crossings in LA, did he? Besides, I was a witness. Millie's death was definitely an accident. I hoped.

My Gold insidious chromosome was now up and running. "For the sake of discussion, would you kill for a million dollars?"

Harold laughed. "I'm too devious for that." He hung up before I could question him further.

An accident, I thought. As it turned out, the next death was no accident. It was deliberate.

18.

I can't say life returned to normal during the week of Millie's candle. Moved to the mantelpiece over our gas log it burned like a reminder of bad dreams. I made daily calls to the LA Missing Persons' office in search of Sarah. Finally the clerk got tired of being pestered and reassured me that they had my number. If they found out anything they'd call and would I please not?

The memorial wick was down to the last inch of wax at the bottom of the flickering blue glass holder when the phone rang. Deborah had just sat down to a dinner of my spinach lasagna, a tasty meal with no meat. Deborah has vegetarian tendencies, though I occasionally tempt her with a steak.

Deborah's clients make the assumption that she's a doctor who is always on call. It's not unusual to be awakened at two in the morning by someone who had a nightmare and wants instant analysis. I've told her to engage an answering service to take the calls that interrupt dinner, but she's too conscientious.

Deborah should have a web site and a 900 number as an on line therapist. We'd make a fortune. At least those on-line horoscope con artists do. Deborah is not a con artist. I'll leave that to the Gold side of the family.

To spare Deborah I picked up the phone. "Yes?"

"It's Arthur."

I didn't recognized the voice. "Arthur who?" This was beginning to sound like a knock-knock joke.

"Arthur, Calumet City, the Gents, your cousin."

"Hi, Arthur. How's tricks?" It was a deliberate reference to the likelihood that besides pushing watered liquor on the tourists he might be a pimp.

"Not so good. I'm worried about this family business."

"What family business?"

"Aunt Sadie's estate."

"What's to worry? You'll outlive us all, Arthur. When you're ninety you'll be rich."

"I'm not worried about the money." It sounded like he was calling from his office at the Gents club. Loud music was playing in the background. I recognized the strains of Night Train, stripper music. Boom. Off come the gloves. Boom, off goes the bra. Boom, boom. "Could you drive over here? We need to talk."

Odd. When he got on that plane in LA he looked like he could kill me himself. Maybe that was his plan. Lure me to Calumet City so his patrons could beat me to death in the gutter, then drag me across the street so the Illinois cops would have to solve it.

It wasn't such a remote possibility. "Can't we just discuss it over the phone?" Over the phone I was safe.

"I'd rather not. Things have been happening."

Now I was curious. Arthur seemed genuinely disturbed. I didn't peg him for being an actor. "What things?"

"Can you come?"

Deborah was curious. "Who is it?"

"My cousin Arthur. He wants me to see him in Calumet City."

"When?" she asked.

"When?" I repeated.

"Can you come tomorrow? Leave early and we can talk at lunch. Cecile will join us. She'd like to get out of the house. I know a great place. Middle eastern food."

I had met Arthur's wife Cecile only once or twice. Maybe at one of the family gatherings at Michiana Shores. Would I know her if I saw her? I wondered how far it was to Calumet City from Lansing. I begged off. "It's a long drive for a lunch date."

"It'll take you about three hours on the interstate," Arthur said. "Put your pedal to the metal."

Some of his customers must be truck drivers. No doubt Arthur had a heavy foot. I wonder what he drove? A white vintage convertible would suit his temperament. "I don't know if my old Volvo can make it. It almost didn't start at the airport when I got back from Sadie's funeral. I wouldn't want to break down in Gary." They were lame excuses, but I didn't want to go.

"Jesus, Adam, don't make me beg."

Considering the truck traffic around Chicago, Arthur's three hours would be at least four for me. It was too far to drive there and back in one day. I turned him down. I regret it now. It's one of those what if situations. What if I had gone the next day as he requested? What difference would it have made? "If it's too private to discuss on the phone, why don't you just send me a letter?"

Arthur lost his temper. He let out a stream of invective he must have learned from that variety of clientele who frequent his dive. If words could kill, I'd have been dead on the spot. He cursed me in English, Yiddish, Polish, I think even a little Arabic. Must have picked it up from a waiter at that middle eastern restaurant. I'm not fluent in Arabic curses. Then he hung up.

I went back to my spinach lasagna, which was now cold. "He was pissed," I said. The curses rang in my ears, killing the taste of the food. "Funny character. One minute he's all hate. The next it's 'Dear old cousin Adam, won't you come for lunch?'"

Deborah sipped her decaf. She never drinks caffeinated coffee at dinner. Keeps her awake. "Sounds like he's bipolar."

Bipolar. That's Deborah's meal ticket. From what little Deborah reveals about her clients, I'd say most of them are bipolar. My layman's understanding of bipolar is a kind of erratic bouncing from high energy excited to depressed and hostile. They used to call it manic. "Isn't everyone?" I asked..

Deborah launched into her lecture mode. "About eight percent of Americans are bipolar. It's because of historic immigration patterns. The people who came to this continent were misfits who didn't get along in their own countries. It's a genetic thing, like Australia, where so many of the people are descended from convicts."

This was familiar territory. "So you think criminality is genetic?"

She put down her cup. "Most behavior is learned, Adam, but certain temperaments are more prone than others."

"Bipolar," I said. I got up to fetch the dessert, a nice strawberry-rhubarb pie I picked up at Econo foods. "That explains why outbursts like the Columbine shooting happen in the United States, but not in other countries. Then the Gold chromosome is just another example. We're all bipolar, you're saying."

"More or less. The Golds are a special case."

I returned with two servings of the strawberry-rhubarb. If I brought the whole pie to the table I might be tempted to take seconds. "So cousin Arthur is bipolar. OK. That gives me an excuse not to go visit. Bipolarity might be catching."

"I doubt it." Deborah studied her piece of pie. "Do we have any ice cream?"

"Fat free frozen yogurt," I said, but I wasn't going to fetch it. "If you don't watch your figure, I might watch someone else's."

"Just so you do nothing but look," Deborah said, and took up her fork.

Deborah and I had settled in front of the TV to watch the weekly British mystery on channel 13 when Arthur's wife, Cecile, called back. I had no reason to believe it was someone else, someone posing as her to lure me away from my home turf, but suspicion is par when you're dealing with the Gold chromosome. I had never spoken with Arthur's wife before and knew her only as a name alongside his in my address book. I sent them an annual Rosh Hashanah card, our only contact, and it was usually one way. Cecile apologized for Arthur's outburst and begged me to visit. If the drive was too tiring I could stay overnight. Couldn't I bring Deborah?

I'd had a nice meal. The dishes were clinking merrily in the dishwasher. By then the heat of Arthur's invective had cooled and I was in an affable mood. It was a weak moment which I now regret. Deborah said she'd come along to keep me from falling asleep at the wheel. We could go in her car. Arthur had been urgent in his demand. He wanted me to see him the next day. I agreed, providing we could wait until Deborah was free. We'd see Arthur and Cecile on Saturday. Saturday, it turned out, was too late.

19.

Cecile suggested we pick her up at their home in Hobart, Indiana, which is more or less on the way to Calumet City. Then, to avoid the crowded I-94, she'd guide us herself through back roads to Arthur's Gent's club. All we had to do was find Hobart. We left Lansing after breakfast.

By the time we got to Gary the trucks on the interstate were lined up like impatient elephants, nose to tail, farting diesel exhaust. Because of the wear and tear on those major arteries the road is under continuous repair. We were caught in a center lane for what seemed like miles of stop and go between a gasoline truck on our left and a monster loaded with coils of steel on the right. If we did have an accident the air bags in the Camry wouldn't help much. Flattened by the steel, incinerated by the gasoline. Good thing I don't bite my fingernails or I'd have chewed down to the second knuckle. If that's possible this was worse than Los Angeles.

Deborah has more guts on the freeways than I have. She has a heavy foot and revels in the ability of her nimble car to accelerate out of trouble. By contrast my sluggish Volvo is built so if you do have an accident you can survive. I found the exit we wanted on the map but eighteen wheelers blocked our view of those big green signs. When we approached the exit we were still in the center lane. Deborah just stopped and refused to move until someone let us out. Then she goosed the Camry through a slot defined by orange plastic traffic cones. We'd escaped. I could dispense with fears of going up in flames. The rest of the run into Hobart was easy.

Hobart, Indiana is a nice little town in the flatlands south east of Chicago. Nice, neat streets. The only cautionary note in this suburban tranquillity were the "neighborhood crime watch" signs posted on every block. Arthur and Cecile had a modest split level with a two car garage in a middle class neighborhood. You can date a home by what siding was in fashion when it was built or remodeled. Arthur's was new enough to have pale green vinyl siding. A boat trailer with about a sixteen foot blue flake runabout was parked in the driveway. I noticed that the outboard motor was chained and padlocked to the transom and one wheel was off the trailer, probably to prevent theft.

Hobart might be at the outer edge of the Chicago megapolis, but not as crime free as one might hope. At least in Hobart you didn't have to imprison yourself behind barred windows and concertina wire as I'd seen in some parts of Los Angeles.

Cecile and Arthur's front door was painted an electric blue. I remembered his gaudy jacket. That blue was not a good combination with the pale green siding, a clash of one person's affinity over decorator's choice. Arthur's home did not have a reinforced screen like Sarah's apartment in California.

Cousin Arthur did have a blue mezuzah nailed to the right doorpost. Mezuzahs are on the doorposts of Jewish homes in recollection of the tenth plague in Egypt. At the time of the exodus the sign on the doorpost was blood, supposed to keep away the angel of death. I hoped it also worked against burglars.

I couldn't remember when I'd seen Arthur's wife Cecile. She had brilliant white hair teased high. Her two piece outfit was classy but gaudy, something you might find on someone in show business with star aspirations. She didn't look like a hooker, mind you, but she'd be at ease in a club with a piano bar and a torch singer. She wore a necklace of brilliant blue beads.

"Nice necklace," I commented.

"Yeh," she said. "Arthur gave it to me. His favorite color."

Deborah and I stood uncomfortably in the entry way. I looked past Cecile into the living room. She had laid a pathway of plastic to protect the carpet. The couches were covered in plastic, too. This was PVC heaven. I hoped she and Arthur weren't allergic to plastic. "Nice place."

"You got time for coffee?"

"We're a little late," Deborah said. "The traffic..."

"I'll just get my coat," Cecile said.

The phone rang. "I hope it's not my neighbor," she said, irritated. "Ollie's such a snoop. Probably saw your car and wants to know who's visiting." Irritated at the interruption Cecile picked up. "Yeh?" Cecile's face was like a kaleidoscope of emotion. It went from irritation to joy, to surprise, then horror. "Oh, my God! Did you call the fire department? Get out of there. To hell with that stuff. Isn't the safe fireproof? Just get out!"

Before we could ask, Cecile explained, "The Club's on fire. Arthur's in the upstairs office. We've got to get there right away."

We jumped in the Camry, me in the back seat with Cecile in front to guide Deborah through the back roads to Calumet City. I couldn't help remembering my fear of being incinerated by a gasoline truck on the interstate. I hoped some similar fate wasn't happening to my cousin Arthur.

20.

Arthur wasn't kidding when he told me the Gent's Club was on the state line. That's even the name of the street; one side Indiana, the other Illinois. The Gent's is on the Indiana side. A string of watering places and topless bars runs up and down both sides of State Line street. Except for the early morning hard line drinkers or hangers on from the night before I wouldn't expect much action at lunch time. There was.

Three fire trucks had the street blocked off and we had to park a block away. Hoses, squirting water at their connectors, snaked across the wet pavement. Cecile stepped over them gingerly in her spike heels. I wondered, if your fire is in Indiana, can you hook up a fire hose in Illinois? And who pays the bill? Must be pretty complicated, living on the edge.

Whatever jurisdictional complications they might be subject to, the firemen were efficient. By the time we arrived it looked like everything was under control. A couple of firemen were rolling up one of the hoses. "Must be out already," I commented.

There was only a wisp of smoke coming from a broken upstairs window. Like his front door at home, the Gent's Club electric sign was blue. It was intact, and there was no outward sign of serious damage. It didn't look like much of a fire. A fireman with an ax was up on the roof.

The local television people had wasted no time. A white truck with folding dish antennas on the roof was parked across the street. Someone lugging a heavy camera was busy with the viewfinder. "I guess it'll all be on the six o'clock news," I said.

I scanned the faces of the onlookers. There were about a dozen standing on the Illinois side of the street. I was hoping Arthur would be among them, watching the crew save his business. One bleary-eyed kid with pierced lips like some cannibal stood on the sidewalk holding his glass of beer. You'd think someone old enough to drink would have more sense than to wear hardware in his mouth. Beside him was a pale B girl wearing a windbreaker and spike heels but possibly nothing else. She was pale. Her makeup was chosen for harsh artificial light. Out of doors she looked like she had just emerged from hibernation and was seeing daylight for the first time. I didn't see Arthur.

Then I spotted the ambulance.

Cecile gasped, "Oh, God," and rushed up to an older fireman who seemed to be supervising. "My husband's in there. He phoned from his office upstairs. Did he get out?"

The fireman in his bizarre uniform looked like something out of the Power Rangers kiddy show except in his case the jacket and helmet were soiled and much worn. He held a portable radio to his ear. "One casualty," he said. "They're bringing him out now."

Cecile bit her lip and kept mumbling, "Oh God, Oh God."

Two firemen emerged from the front door of the Gent's club wearing breathing apparatus. I had seen a TV report on the new device invented so you can spot bodies in thick smoke. The first fireman had on one of those. Between them they carried an unconscious form.

The fireman prevented Cecile from rushing forward. "Stay back, lady. Go stand over there behind the fire line."

We followed her around the parked fire trucks and past the onlookers on the other side of the street to the ambulance, but the paramedical crew were so quick we didn't get a chance to see who it was being hustled away. I had this feeling of deja vu. Less than a week ago I was following another ambulance, that one with Millie. First Millie, now Arthur.

"We'll follow it," Deborah said, taking charge. She hustled Cecile back to the car but by the time we got to it we had no idea where the ambulance had gone.

By then Cecile was hysterical. Deborah got her into the Camry. "Take it easy, Cecile." Calming people down was Deborah's department. She put her arms around Cecile and whispered to her. "You don't know if that was Arthur they brought out. Even if it was, you don't know his condition." She turned to me. "Adam, find out where the ambulance went."

Traffic had been diverted. I walked down the middle of State Line street back to the scene of the fire. The sight of someone, probably my cousin, being taken off in an ambulance reminded me of Millie. That wasn't even a week ago and again here I was at the scene of tragedy. This shouldn't be happening. People would start thinking I was the angel of death.

I caught the fire chief as he was climbing into the cab of his truck. "Where would the ambulance be going? I think the victim is my cousin Arthur Gold. He owns the Gent's Club."

"Probably St. Vincent's," The fire chief said. He took off his helmet, revealing a shock of gray hair. "He'll have to answer some questions of the arson squad. This fire was no accident."

"How do you know that?" I asked.

"Found a gasoline can on the stairs outside the office door. Looks like someone had a grudge against the Gent's club."

"Maybe some customer got mad because he was served a watered down drink," I suggested, but I couldn't help but wonder if dear Aunt Sadie's million dollar prize had something to do with it.

The fire chief gave me directions to the hospital. Deborah handed me her car keys. "You drive. I'll take care of Cecile."

21.

It was Arthur they had taken out of the Gent's and he was in bad shape. They wouldn't let us in to see him while they worked on him in the ER, so we waited in the hallway.

We weren't alone there. Emergency rooms are the last resort of people without health insurance. The waiting spaces for them are a limbo of worry. We sat an hour before a doctor came out to report that Arthur wasn't badly burned but had to go to intensive care for smoke inhalation.

We couldn't get into the IC unit, either.

I tried to question Cecile while we waited near the IC. I knew nothing about the operation of night clubs. "Does Arthur usually go to the club on Saturdays?"

Cecile was so distraught it was hard to get an answer out of her. She caught her breath and blew her nose with a tissue. "He didn't plan to go because we were going out for lunch with you, but then he got a call from someone to go down to the club."

"Who was it?"

"No idea."

"There's no window in Arthur's office," Cecile explained. "He was trapped in there. That's when he called the fire department and me."

Deborah had her arm around Cecile. I noticed that she had kept physical contact with Cecile ever since we left the fire. Deborah didn't want me to ask all those questions, but I had to know.

"Did anyone else know we were coming to visit?"

Cecile wrinkled her forehead. "I don't know. Is that important?"

"Arthur said he had to see me urgently. He didn't explain. Has he had any threats? Anything odd happening lately?"

"My neighbor, Ollie, said something. She's been watching the neighborhood like a hawk ever since someone stole her extension ladder. Ollie's that snoopy one who phoned and wanted to know who you were. I try not to pay any attention to her. She's one of those people who gets bored with housework and drops in without an invitation, wanting coffee and company. She means well."

"Maybe we should talk to her," I suggested.

It wasn't a smile, but Cecile's sarcastic smirk showed she was coming out of her hysteria. "She'd be glad to. She'll talk your legs off."

Millie's death, so far as I could tell, was an accident. I was pretty sure it was just a coincidence that Yahya Ragani the rug merchant had also done business with Schmuel and Sylvia. The fire at the Gent's was deliberate. It wasn't a coincidence that Arthur was inside the club when it was torched. Someone had lured him there. If they wanted to make this death look like an accident, they'd done a sloppy job of it.

I remembered that Harold said a murderer couldn't inherit. If Arthur died, Miriam, Schmuel, Jake, Harold and I were the last on Aunt Sadie's list. Sarah had gone into the river. Millie was hit by a car. Now Arthur was in the wrong place when a fire was started. I vowed to be extra careful when crossing streets in front of Iranian rug dealers and to always have an escape route in case of fire. I hoped nobody else in the family was accident prone.

Schmuel was in California. He couldn't have started the fire. I couldn't imagine Miriam murdering her own brother or my brother Harold lighting anything except his cigar. But Jake, my gangster cousin, was in Chicago. That wasn't far. Jake could have engineered what I'd heard him call "Greek lightning." That snake. If I had to play the part of mongoose, it would be a dangerous game. Sometimes the mongoose gets the cobra. Sometimes the cobra wins.

For now I would postpone that confrontation. I needed more evidence. Maybe Cecile's nosy, boring neighbor knew something.

22.

The hospital staff wouldn't let Cecile into the IC unit to see Arthur so we persuaded her to come out with us and grab a bite of lunch. She pointed out the hole in the wall middle eastern restaurant that Arthur frequented and we went there. The store front was barely wide enough to accommodate the name of the place: Amman Middle Eastern Cafe. The sign on the window offered a take out menu which was just as well, for inside we found only four tables. The one at the back near the kitchen was available.

The owner was Jordanian, maybe a Palestinian. More than half of the Jordanians are. The owner himself waited on us. He was a swarthy guy with a clean apron and a Semitic nose. I didn't know how he'd feel with a bunch of Jews in his place, but he recognized Cecile. "Ah, Mrs. Gold. Where's Arthur, today?"

We had hoped to distract Cecile by taking her to the restaurant. Now she started bawling again.

Deborah explained there was a fire at the club and Arthur was in the hospital.

"Terrible, terrible," the Jordanian said and handed us menus. They were done on a computer-- a nice graphic of a middle-eastern skyline, possibly Jerusalem-- and slid into transparent plastic sleeves. Amman Middle Eastern cafe served an American breakfast special at all hours. No matter when you staggered out of one of those Cal City dives you could still get breakfast. Two eggs, bacon, toast, three bucks. Such a deal. I saw that the owner was Jamal Fridoon.

"Are you Mr. Fridoon?"

"Yes, yes. Call me Jamal. This is America."

Most of the items I didn't recognize. I looked over the top of the menu and asked. "Jamal, you have any idea who might have torched Arthur's place?"

"Torched?"

"Set fire to."

Jamal spread his hands in a universal sign of helplessness. "What do I know? This is not a good neighborhood."

"There's no protection racket going here, is there?"

Jamal wasn't familiar with the concept. "Protection?"

"Tough guys demand a weekly payment in cash in case your place might have a fire. That is, if you don't pay you do have a fire. Anything like that going on here in Calumet City?"

"No. Nothing like that."

It was a long shot, but I had to ask. "Arthur came here often. Did he ever say anything about troubles in the business? Anybody who might have a grudge against Arthur?"

"I don't know."

Jamal was nervous and I suspected he wasn't a good liar. Maybe I hadn't asked the right question. Probably this wasn't the best time.

Deborah and I ordered falafels, but Cecile just wanted a cup of soup. She had no appetite.

The falafel was better than I'd found in Lansing. Arthur had discovered a good place. I only hoped he would be able to continue to frequent the Amman Middle Eastern cafe.

When I went to the cash register to pay the bill I asked Jamal, "Do you have a business card? I'd like to call you some other time when it's more convenient."

"Truly, Mr. Gold..."

"Rottman," I corrected. "Adam Rottman. I'm Arthur's cousin from Michigan."

"Mr. Rottman, then. Truly, I don't know anything about the fire or Arthur's business. Sometimes we make a few jokes about Israelis and Palestinians. I teach him to swear in Arabic. Nothing else."

So I was right about the Arabic curses.

The business cards were beside the cash register. I took one. Maybe if I knew how or what to ask Jamal Fridoon I might get the answers I was looking for.

23.

Cecile wanted to go back to the hospital. That could take days and we had no intention of staying overnight. I did want to question her nosy neighbor, though. If we could find the way back ourselves we might try her. Might get a clue to the fire.

We hadn't paid attention to the short cut from Hobart to Calumet City that Cecile showed Deborah. Cecile drew a tiny map on the back of a gasoline credit receipt. We returned her to the hospital.

"How will you get home?" Deborah asked through her open window.

Cecile brightened. "I can take Arthur's car. It's usually parked behind the club."

"Just so you're not stranded."

We followed the instructions and found our way back to Hobart. Arthur and Cecile's street was quiet. The house next door was older than theirs. Instead of the obligatory picture window in front with a prominent lamp on display, the neighbor's place had a bay window on the ground floor and matching one on the second floor. A pick-up camper stood on its stilts on the grass beside the driveway. Obviously Hobart didn't have a law against people flaunting boats, campers, RV's and other toys. Some towns do.

A sticker on Cecile's neighbor's front door said "Operation Identification. All valuables engraved and registered with the police." Ollie was reluctant to open the door until Deborah explained that there had been a fire at The Gent's Club and Arthur was in the hospital. Eager for the gossip, Ollie let us in.

She was a plump, middle-aged woman with a round face and dimples at the corners of her mouth. She reminded me of the Pillsbury dough boy, a figure that makes you want to poke a finger into her and see if she giggles. I restrained myself.

"Cup of coffee?" Ollie announced and went to fetch a tray with a plate of home made chocolate chip cookies, a pot of coffee that had been kept warm in the kitchen, and three mugs. Apparently she collected them, for there were mugs all over the place. At least you could drink out of them. Amazing how people collect useless stuff-- Beany Babies, old outboard motors, fishing reels, dolls. It must be a national disease that goes with the bipolarity Deborah harps on. I'm not a collector. For me one Raggedy Ann is more than plenty.

Among the mugs displayed on the window sill in the living room was a pair of binoculars. There was no bird feeder on the lawn. This Ollie really was a snoop.

I waited patiently until I could get a word in. "I hear you're an active participant in the Neighborhood Crime Watch. We saw the signs."

"Oh yes. With so many couples both working there aren't many of us homemakers around to keep an eye on things in the middle of the day. That's when the thieves get to work. Someone stole our ladder and used it to get into a house a couple of blocks away. We got the ladder back because our name and address is painted on it. The crooks pretended to be painters, stole our ladder, then used it to get into an open second story window." Her eyes narrowed. "I keep a watch now. Nothing gets past me."

"Then you'd know if anyone was casing the neighborhood, particularly if they were checking out Cecile and Arthur's place."

"I think so," Ollie said.

"Has there been any suspicious activity?"

Ollie thought for a long moment. She poured herself a refill from the glass coffee-maker pot she'd brought with her from the kitchen. "Yes. A van parked across the street one afternoon last week. White, but no signs on it or anything. I didn't see if there was anyone inside. Those tinted windows, you know. It was there past supper time, but when we got ready to go to bed it was gone."

I remembered the binoculars on her window sill. "Did you by any chance get the license number?"

She appreciated my perception. Maybe she thought I was a snoop, too. "The van was facing the wrong way. The front plate was one of those fun things. Chicago Bears, it said."

I commented, "Someone's a football fan."

"Everyone around here is a football fan, Mr. Rottman."

I stopped her before she launched a play by play of the Thanksgiving day game. "Did the van park there more than once?"

She couldn't be sure.

"If they really were casing the neighborhood they didn't necessarily have to be checking on the Golds. They could have been keeping an eye on several houses. Where were they parked?"

Ollie pointed across the street.

"Could have been the IRS looking for tax evaders," I quipped, then, remembering the nature of the clubs in Cal City, almost added "or the vice squad" but thought the better of it.

"Oh, my!" Ollie looked guilty. Maybe she and her husband fiddled their taxes, like everyone else. "Do you think they would? The IRS, I mean?"

Deborah interjected. "I don't think so."

"You could use a telescope," I suggested, then quickly added, "for the crime watch."

Ollie pointed at the ceiling. "Upstairs."

I had noticed the bay window on the second floor. I must remember to draw our curtains back in Lansing in case we have an Ollie in our neighborhood, too.

Deborah gave me a stealthy wink. "Thanks for the coffee Ollie. You keep your eyes open. If you see anything suspicious, tell Cecile. When Arthur gets out of the hospital he may be laid up for quite a while. Whoever torched his club might make another attempt."

Ollie's eyes widened nearly as big as her coffee mug. "Do you think there'd be a drive by shooting?"

"Let's hope not."

"When will Arthur get out of the hospital?" Ollie asked.

"First he has to survive," I said. "Considering the past couple of weeks in the Gold family..." I left the sentence unfinished. I didn't want to tell the whole story. It would occupy that busybody snoop for weeks. If she knew about Sadie, Sarah, Millie and the tontine she'd tell the entire town. With embellishments the story could become monumental. If she pestered other neighbors as much as she did Cecile, the woman was a walking, talking grocery store tabloid. "We have to get going. It's a long drive home. Thanks for the coffee. I appreciate your time."

We left, stopping on the front steps as Ollie's door shut and was latched behind us. We took a joint, deep sigh of relief.

"She's a voyeur," Deborah said. "Dollars to donuts."

"That's one thing I wouldn't bet on."

Deborah paused with her key in the lock of the Camry and talked to me across the roof. "You were baiting her, weren't you? About the IRS stalking people. Admit it."

I feigned innocence. "Just a little gentle mischief, Maybe it's the Gold chromosome." I had an idea. "Talking about mischief, let's stop at the cottage in Michiana. See if the movers have brought Sarah's stuff. We can do a little snooping of your own. It's more or less on our way, a few miles off the I-94."

"You're suspicious of Harold, aren't you? Think he wants to hock Sarah's collection?"

"I don't think so, not as long as she's just missing. We don't know for sure that she's dead. I keep hoping she's in Mexico or someplace."

"That's wishful thinking, Adam. I think she is dead, and someone killed her. Someone in the Gold family."

"Now you're the one who's teasing. Trying to scare me. It's not fair. As a psychologist you have the advantage."

When we got in the car and buckled up she asked, "Do you have a key to the cottage?"

"My old key is at home someplace, but I know where one used to be hidden. I don't know if Harold has changed the locks since he bought the place from our folks."

Deborah looked at her watch. "We'll still be in Lansing in time for supper. What's cooking?"

I hadn't a clue. "Leftovers," I said to kill that line of thought. "I'll think about supper while you drive. Let's go see if the Raggedy Anns have arrived." What I was really wishing for was that my missing sister would be there along with her dolls. You're not supposed to tell your wishes, my mother always said, or they don't come true.

24.

After we got east of Gary the traffic lightened up and when we turned off for Michigan City on highway 421 there was none. Once we passed the shopping mall at the south side of the city it was like driving into a ghost town. I hadn't been there in years. Franklin Street, the main drag, had been remodeled with brick pavement and planters in an attempt to revitalize the place but it was too late. The mall at the edge of the city had sucked away all the business and the downtown had an air of bankruptcy with empty store fronts and a lack of shoppers. Sears was gone and the old South Shore railway station closed. Its passengers were commuters to Chicago and needed more parking than the old location offered. The movie was closed, beaten into oblivion by the multiplex at the mall.

I directed Deborah to the Lake Michigan shore, and we drove along the road that had once been so familiar. When we were kids Harold and I used to ride the bus from Stop Forty down to the harbor and fish off the breakwater. Some of the old cottages remained, but things were turning upscale.

Lake Michigan's water level was low and the sandy beach broad. Some years, when the water was high, the autumn storms took out those houses built on the beach, which is why our parents had built on the side of the road away from the lake. The road was a buffer and when the house across from us was washed away, our view of sunsets improved. That was before the Sears tower was built, then the world's tallest, and we could actually see across the lake as far as Chicago from the living room.

The Rottman cottage is up on what must at one time have been a sandy ridge but is all landscaped and stable now. The garage is underneath, dug into the bank, and you can enter the house by going upstairs from it, which gets you into the basement. It's convenient when unloading groceries in the rain.

Compared to California with its palm trees and lush vegetation, Michiana was still wintry and deserted. It would be a couple of months before the summer crowd returned, mothers with their babies lugging chairs, coolers, towels, and blankets down to the beach, grannies with their beach chairs set up at the water's edge so they could cool their feet and their tuchases. Those days when Harold, little Sarah and I lay about in endless leisure were long past.

Deborah parked off the road in front of the garage. Out of old habit I checked the mail box, found a flyer for after Christmas sales. Sand had blown up from the beach, but someone had swept enough of it away to get the garage door open. "Looks like someone's been here," I said, then climbed the outside steps to the house. They were steeper than I remembered. My legs were younger then. I wondered how Harold managed them with his three hundred pounds and emphysema.

The blinds were all drawn except up on the second story in front. "Where's the key hidden?" Deborah asked.

"By the back door, under a brick," I said. The walk to the back of the house was paved with bricks and we used to hide a key under one of them, but which? It had been a long time.

I lifted each of the loose bricks. No key. Then I inspected the lock at the back door. "It looks like the old lock," I said. "My key back home probably fits. Too bad I didn't think about this before we left."

"Won't Harold be angry if he finds out you were snooping around the place?"

"He doesn't have to know." She was right. Harold had a temper. If not angry Harold could be irritated. He liked to run things himself. "I have a standing invitation." That was my excuse to Deborah. It might not wash with Harold.

We couldn't see in any of the ground floor windows. "The garage has a window," I remembered. It was in the corner that stuck out from the bank. It provided some natural light, but was awkward to get to. I scooted down the steep bank on my bottom to peek through the garage window.

A pair of eyes were staring back at me, vacant, innocent, dead eyes. For an instant I thought I'd seen a corpse. The face, the braids, reminded me of Sarah and her ridiculous costume. My secret wish had not been granted. Sarah was not at the cottage. The face in the window was Raggedy Ann. In the semi-darkness behind that doll were scores more. "The movers have been here," I announced. "Harold must have driven up from Indianapolis to let them in."

"He could have told you," Deborah said as we got back to the car.

"Brother Harold doesn't tell me everything."

"Only what he wants you to know."

As an afterthought I checked the garbage can. Down in the bottom were empty wrappers from McDonald's-- two large soda cups, a coffee cup, three large fries, the assorted fast food trash that is filling the landfills of the world. "Someone's been here. Probably the movers."

"Well done, Mr. Detective," Deborah said. "Now see if you can brush all that sand off your butt before you get it over my nice upholstery."

When we got back to Lansing I'd call Cecile to see how Arthur was doing in the hospital. Then I'd call Harold and give him the news of the latest Gold mishap. I wondered how he'd react if I told him we'd been at the cottage.

25.

I decided not to call Harold until I heard from Cecile, then had a hard time reaching her. I left messages twice on their answering machine. Hobart, Indiana is on Central time, Lansing, Michigan on Eastern. We had driven about eight hours to Calumet City and back with the Michigan City detour and were tired. Deborah and I went to bed early.

It was nearly midnight when the phone rang. I was asleep. Normally, to avoid Deborah's crazy clients, we turn off the ringer. There's nothing like having an insomniac phone you in the middle of the night to force you to share her experience. We usually let the answering machine save our sleep, but in this case I didn't want to miss Cecile's call. I jumped up, hoping Deborah could sleep through.

It was Cecile, apologizing for the hour. The news of Arthur was not good. In spite of getting oxygen for his smoke-damaged lungs Arthur had suffered a cardiac arrest and though the doctors revived his heart, he was in a coma.

I stood by the phone barefoot and chilled in my pajamas. The thermostat had shut down the heat for the night. "Was he conscious at all?"

"No. I don't know what to do, Adam. What if he's brain dead?"

I shared her unspoken vision of cousin Arthur lying for years in limbo between life and death, with life support machines, feeding tubes, the mounting medical bills that would bankrupt all but Bill Gates. I imagined Arthur lingering for years as the cousins died off until there were only two left, Arthur and one other survivor who crept into the hospital and pulled the plug to get the prize, Aunt Sadie's million smackers.

I was certain that wouldn't happen. Not the part about pulling the plug, but about Arthur's living very long in a vegetative state. Another Gold gone. How many to go? Five.

It still seemed safe. If someone was out to eliminate the cousins for the money I had a one in five chance of being next. Better than one in two.

I was reminded of that Agatha Christie play, "Ten Little Indians," a classic manor house drawing room drama where the characters are represented by little Indian statues on the mantelpiece until one by one the characters and the statues dwindle to one. Except there weren't ten Golds. Counting Sarah, we were only seven.

Correction, had been only seven. Sarah was missing. Millie was dead. It looked like the final curtain for Arthur in this family drama. "If he is brain dead and there's no hope, what will you do?" I asked, knowing the answer already.

"Pull the plug."

"What about the Gent's club? Can you run that business on your own?" Equal opportunity sentiments notwithstanding, I have to admit that handling bartenders, B-girls, and bouncers seemed an unsuitable job for a woman.

"Insurance should cover the fire damage. Cousin Jake once told Arthur he can always find a buyer for it if we want to sell."

"Jake?" I was surprised.

Cecile explained. "He advises Arthur sometimes. Arthur says Jake has good connections."

I supposed there were some aspects to running the Gent's Club that were best kept within the family, like fronting for prostitution and drugs.

Jake might have a double motive for getting rid of Arthur. Besides being a step closer to Sadie's fortune, he could pick up the Gent's Club for a bargain price. "What will you do, if Arthur...?" I didn't want to add "dies."

"I can go back to hostessing at the steak house."

Cecile would be good at that. She has the appearance, the poise, and is at ease among strangers. "Let me know if there's anything I can do," I said, not having a clue.

"I've always avoided Jake. He gives me the creeps. Maybe you could call him for me."

It wasn't something I'd look forward to-- Jake my gangster cousin of the pin stripe suit with shoulder pads and elevated shoes. He could have engineered the Greek lightning job. I couldn't see

Jake bound by family loyalties. I hoped there wasn't a white van parked across our street, stalking us.

"I suppose I could... if necessary." I had never been to Jake's house. I knew it was north of Chicago in Deerfield, Grandpa's upscale neighborhood. Deerfield was even farther north than Skokie where Jews fled as blacks moved into Hyde Park where my mother grew up. If driving the I-94 gauntlet to Hobart and Calumet City had been unpleasant, going all the way through Chicago to Deerfield would be horrendous.

"Let's hope it won't be necessary," I said. "Let's pray that Arthur recovers and your life gets back to normal."

"I don't think our life has ever been normal," Cecile said. "Arthur used to work most of the night and sleep half the day. Owning a strip club is like a perpetual night shift."

"Get some sleep, Cecile," I suggested. "Call me any time."

I hung up the phone and shut off the ringer. One call like that was enough. Worried, I put on my slippers and took a walk through the house. Everything was quiet. The kitchen clock made its little clucking sound. The refrigerator cycled on. I stood in the front window and looked out at the street. The only light out there was way down at the corner, but I could see an unfamiliar vehicle parked under a tree. It was a large van, almost as big as one of those ugly SUV's that bully their way in the traffic. I hadn't seen it before. It was white.

I lowered the venetian blind, then felt foolish about it. I had not turned on the lights. Nobody could see me, standing there in my PJ's, watching the street. Or could they? And if they could, who cared?

It was too chilly to be standing around. I went back to bed.

Deborah was half asleep. She roused herself enough to ask, "Who was it?"

"Cecile."

"News?"

"Coma. Maybe brain dead."

"Poor Cecile," she murmured, and went back to sleep.

I didn't. I lay awake a long time wondering what I'd have to say to Jake if I did have to meet with him. Maybe Harold would have a suggestion. I'd call him in the morning.

26.

When I got up to make our breakfast I checked to see if the van was still there. It was gone. I didn't tell Deborah about it. She'd only suggest I was imagining things.

Off she went to her office leaving me to my housespousery. Standing in the laundry room I thought about having a new business card printed in case people at parties asked what I do for a living. "Adam Rottman, Home maker. Cooking, general chores, laundry. I don't do windows."

I'd make one more try with the LA Missing Persons office before calling Harold, which meant I waited until noon, Michigan time. There was no news of Sarah. Nobody had found her body. For once the Missing Persons person had a constructive suggestion: had the LA Times run a story on her with a picture? That might help.

It was worth a try. I called the LA Times. The switch board put me on to a reporter and I wrote down the name and extension number. Tompkins, Liz Tompkins. Reporters must get more goofy calls than 911 operators who deal with cats up a tree and "Someone's in my back yard." LA had so many missing persons-- runaways, spouses deserting their families, Alzheimer's patients wandering off-- that The Times had material for a regular daily department.

Editors, aware that rape stories can trigger copycat rapists, don't want to foster a city-wide terror that people are disappearing. It's bad enough that the majority of Americans believe in UFO's, MS Tompkins said. People would panic, claiming aliens had abducted their loved ones. Tinseltown was already full of loonies.

I was certain that Sarah was not abducted by aliens. I tried another angle, told Liz Tompkins about the tontine. That piqued her interest. There was a story in that. Did I have a picture of Sarah?

The best quick source would be Schmuel, so I called his number. Again I got Sylvia and cringed at the sound of her voice when she picked up her phone.

"Yeh? Whaddaya want?"

Bitch. "This is Adam back in Michigan. What have you got, a grudge against people who call you?"

She almost apologized. "I was expecting someone else."

I got right to the point. "The LA Times will run a missing persons piece on Sarah if we can provide a picture of her. Do you have one?"

"Schmuel has one someplace, I'm sure. There were plenty taken at Sadie's ninetieth birthday party. Sarah was the photographer. She's got all that equipment from her bar mitzvah shoots. I remember she used a tripod and got into a couple of group portraits herself."

"The Times could crop her face out of one of those," I suggested.

"Schmuel can probably find a copy."

She didn't sound enthusiastic. I was certain she'd deliberately forget. "This is important, Sylvia. We've got to find Sarah, if she's alive, before someone else gets killed."

"What do you mean, someone else?"

"There's been a fire bombing at cousin Arthur's night club in Calumet City."

"He owns a night club?"

Goes to show how little we cousins knew of each other's lives. I had no idea of Sylvia's life beyond shopping. Judging from her clothes and Schmuel's expensive car they were into conspicuous consumption, an activity not confined, I admitted, to J.A.P.s. "Arthur's in the hospital on life support, in a coma."

Sylvia didn't sound shocked. "Really."

"I'm not making this up, Sylvia. I was there."

"You were there when Millie got killed, too, Adam. Sure you're not a jinx?"

I tried to ignore the insinuation. No point in this conversation turning into a screaming match, not if I expected Sylvia to see to it that Schmuel the schlemiel actually dug up a photo and took it to the LA Times. "Hey, Sylvia, lighten up. Arthur called us himself. Something was troubling him."

"A likely story. Are you sure you don't have blackouts? Like maybe you come to with matches in your pocket and a smell of gasoline on your clothes? I'm glad you live in Michigan, Adam, and not in LA. Lucky your wife is a psychiatrist. Maybe she can cure you."

"Psychologist," I corrected. "And no I do not have blackouts or matches in my pocket. Besides, who said anything about gasoline?"

Suddenly she was defensive. Could loquacious Sylvia, always with a mean comment, be stuck for a retort? Deborah was right. The country is infected with bipolar, hyper misfits. You didn't have to be a Gold by birth to have the chromosome. Maybe being married to Schmuel it rubbed off on Sylvia, like Monsanto spliced genes that escaped.

After a long pause Sylvia changed the subject. "Give me the name of that reporter again."

"Liz Tompkins." I told her the LA Times number and the extension.

"I'll get Schmuel right on it," Sylvia said, suddenly cooperative. "And if you witness any other convenient accidents, you be sure and call us."

"You can count on me."

"And don't have one yourself," Sylvia warned.

She was right. "I'll be extra careful."

The LA police weren't producing any leads to Sarah's disappearance. We had to do what we could on our own. I couldn't be certain that Sylvia would prod Schmuel into delivering Sarah's photo to the LA Times reporter. If we didn't get a story run as news, we could place an ad. I had not given up hope that someone would see her picture and recognize Sarah. She'd be hard to miss. How many crazy women walked around dressed like Raggedy Ann, even in Los Angeles?

27.

After I hung up on Sylvia I called Harold at his law office in Indianapolis. He was with a client, his paralegal told me, but he would call back.

I still hadn't cleaned the living room, but the vacuum is so noisy that I wouldn't hear the phone, so I waited by the picture window, checking out the neighborhood. We don't have those "Neighborhood Crime Watch" signs like Cecile and Arthur have in Hobart. Our part of Lansing is quiet. It helps to live on a cul de sac. It cuts down on the cruising.

That white van was back. It had been gone when I made breakfast, but now it had returned. Too bad I didn't have any binoculars like Cecile's nosy neighbor, Ollie. I thought about just going out, walking up to it, and telling whoever it was to piss off. What if someone rolled down one of those tinted windows and shoved a gun in my face? What would I do then? In all probability, die. Like from fright. If I did go out and check on it, I'd have to be more subtle.

The phone rang. "Yes, Harold."

"You knew it was me. You got caller I.D.?"

"No. I'm telepathic." I launched into my report of yesterday's events, leaving out the detour to the cottage. I didn't want brother Harold to be angry if he thought I was snooping. I added the bit about the LA Times news story.

"Good idea, Adam."

"If a news story doesn't turn up any leads, we can run an ad with Sarah's picture."

"Do you think that's necessary? You'd have to run it every day for at least a week before anyone takes notice. That could be expensive."

That was odd, brother Harold worrying about money. "Sylvia said she didn't know Arthur had a night club, but when I told her about the fire she mentioned gasoline. The firemen found a gas can on the stairs outside Arthur's office, but I didn't mention that to Sylvia."

"So?" Harold sounded like he was eating something. Maybe he did lunch at his desk, brown bagging it or sending out for a sandwich. "What are you getting at? You think Sylvia and Schmuel hired an arsonist?"

"Somebody could have," I said. "I can't see Schmuel flying to Chicago to burn out his cousin. Schmuel couldn't light a barbecue without setting fire to himself. It was probably someone who had a grudge against Arthur. Maybe some pimp mad about one of his stable of girls working the Gent's club. It could have been Jake if he wanted to buy the club cheap and whoever was hired to set the fire didn't know Arthur was inside. Arson is one thing. Arson when someone dies is murder."

"You been studying law, Adam?" Harold's sarcasm was palpable. He liked to flaunt his education.

I tried to match his tone with a sour, "Thanks." In the old days when resumes mattered he used to say my business degree was a trade school diploma. Not that law school is any different.

I did know that Sarah's stuff had been delivered, but I wasn't going to tell him. "When will the movers deliver Sarah's doll collection? You want me to check on them? Someone has to be there."

"It's all taken care of," Harold said.

"I could drive to Michigan City and check." The distance was about the same for both of us, but Harold had his law practice. I just had the laundry.

"Don't bother," Harold said between mouthfuls of whatever.

"What are you eating?" I asked. "You shouldn't talk with your mouth full. You'll choke."

"You're sounding like our mother," Harold said. "I send out for a foot long sandwich. Saves time."

"It wouldn't be a bother to drive over to the cottage," I said. "I'd be glad to, just to make sure the collection is safe."

Harold swallowed and spoke clearly. "I said not to bother, Adam. It's all taken care of."

"Alright, alright. No need to get huffy about it. I'm only offering to help."

"Anything else?" Harold was ready to hang up.

"If Cecile has them pull the plug on Arthur's life support, what do we do about the funeral?"

"You go."

I'd had enough of funerals. "Cecile's neighbor thinks someone was staking out the neighborhood before the fire. A white van, she said. Now there's a white van parked across the street here."

"Vans are common these days. Stop worrying, Adam. Talk to your psychiatrist. Make an appointment with Deborah."

"Psychologist. She's a psychologist." Now I was ready to hang up.

It wasn't a very productive conversation until Harold's last words. "So you think someone put a hit on Arthur?"

"Could be."

Harold had the oddest reaction. He laughed. I didn't know if he was laughing at me for being so paranoid or something else.

That was irritating. I decided that after I did the household chores I'd put together my expenses for the LA trip and send him a bill. He had promised to cover the cost of my search for Sarah. Now I'd hold him to it. It would be nice to have a check before my Visa bill came in.

I was still worried about that suspicious van. We had once observed a lot of nighttime traffic at a house that was supposed to be empty. I suspected drugs. After we called the police, the traffic stopped. It pays to keep an eye on what goes on in your neighborhood. You never know....

28.

I couldn't reach Cecile at her home so left a message on the answering machine. A call to the hospital IC section hit a blank. I might be a relative, but cousins didn't count. The duty nurse wouldn't tell me anything. She did consent to take a message for Cecile if she was there. I didn't have confidence in the nurses' station as a message center for inquiring relatives.

The thought that Jake of the pinstripe suit and elevated shoes might have made a contract for arson unnerved me. What kind of a person could do a thing like that? But Arthur's being caught in the fire could have been an accident. It didn't have to be Jake. It could be an irate customer or a competitor on State Line avenue.

To confront Jake and ask he he had ordered what they call "Greek lightning" would be like walking into the lion's den and asking, 'Did you eat that lamb?' 'Who, me? It was half eaten when I found it.' I couldn't expect an honest answer.

Maybe cooking up something great would take my mind off all this family business. I pondered several menus that would raise my esteem in the annals of housespousery, but each one demanded an ingredient that wasn't in the house. I didn't want to fire up the Volvo for a grocery run if it meant missing a call from Cecile.

The afternoon dragged on. The van was still across the street. I told myself it might belong to a visiting relative of a neighbor, but the tontine thing nagged at me. What was a real possibility was that one of Deborah's clients was stalking her. That's the occupational hazard of dealing with meshugas.

Maybe I should take up a hobby, like Sarah. Collect bird baths or something and spend all my time on E-bay looking for rare ones at a bargain price. I realized I was spending too much time alone in the house. Maybe we should get a cat I could talk to. No wonder some housewives went stir crazy.

To my relief Deborah came home early.

She swept through the front door, swinging her briefcase and smiling. "Adam! There you are."

"Where else would I be? You're home early."

"A couple of cancellations. I thought I'd catch you in a coffee clutch with that nymphet next door."

"That nymphet" she was talking about is a bosomy grad student thirty-five years my junior who once came over to borrow a cup of sugar, kindling memories of days long ago when it might have led to something.

"Shucks, she just left. Next time come home earlier. I promise to wear something sexy."

"Like maybe just an apron and slippers?" Deborah hung up her coat in the closet, checked the mail on the hall table, and asked, "Speaking of aprons, what's for dinner?"

"Nothing yet. Everything I could think of lacked some ingredient and I didn't want to leave in case Cecile called about Arthur's condition."

Deborah gave me a big kiss then held me at arms length. "Adam, how many times do I have to tell you that things are going to happen that you have no control over? You just have to let them be and stop worrying. Go with the flow."

"That's your professional advice?"

"For now. So she didn't call?"

"No. I talked to Sylvia and Harold." I recounted my conversations, including what I left out about the trip to the cottage.

"Let's hit Murray's steak house tonight," Deborah said.

"You?" I asked, surprised. "Eat meat?"

"I've been thinking about steak every since Arthur suggested it, except we got falafel instead."

I made certain the back door dead bolt was thrown while she put on a windbreaker. I made doubly sure the front door was locked.

"Am I seeing signs of compulsive disorder?" Deborah asked, amused and a bit worried.

"Just being careful," I said.

We went in her car. As we passed the van parked across the street I tried to see if someone was inside but the windows were too dark. I was able to see that the front license place said "Chicago

Bears." There must be a lot of such fans about, but did they all drive white vans?

Looking back, however, I saw that the van was pulling out, doing a U-turn, and following us.

I nudged Deborah and suggested she make a couple of turns and see if I was right in my suspicions. I was.

Deborah speeded up.

"What's this? A car chase?" I asked, alarmed.

"You'll see," Deborah said, grinning. She slowed down for a traffic light so she could go through on the yellow, forcing the van to run a red light. It did, narrowly missing someone who had the green. She headed for downtown Lansing and the state capitol building with its skinny dome, Michigan's imitation of the real thing in Washington. The van stayed behind us.

When Deborah pulled up in front of the state police headquarters she blew the horn at the patrol car parked out in front. A state patrolman got out and started toward us.

The van sped by and kept on going.

The patrolman came up to the window. He looked to be at least sixteen. When had he shaved first? Last week? "Can I help you, ma'am?"

"No. Everything's fine now, thank you, officer," Deborah said with a smile that would melt the heart of a hanging judge.

We pulled away. The van was nowhere in sight. "Good move," I said.

"I saw it in a movie once."

"Great!" I said. "Maybe if we rent some Jackie Chan films we could learn martial arts. Pow! Gotcha!" Trouble was, this wasn't a movie, I was no Jackie Chan, and I had no idea who could be stalking me.

29.

Murray's Steak House is a favorite for the more affluent students at Michigan State university. It's where the faculty bring candidates for jobs and parents take their graduating offspring to celebrate the end of tuition. It's a big, noisy place on those occasions and weekends, but quiet enough in the middle of the week. The food is good and plentiful, the price right.

Not in a hurry to go home, we lingered over a couple of T-bones lubricated with Murray's house red wine. As usual, it was too much food so we let the dessert cart go by with its varieties of calorific goodies. It was dark by the time we left.

We had lost whoever was following us downtown, but when we got back the van was parked across the street again in its usual place. This was beginning to get on my nerves.

We have a remote control garage door opener. Deborah pulled in beside my elderly Volvo. The electric door clunked shut behind us.

I got a big flashlight off the work bench. "I'm going to get that bastard's license plate number," I said. "Got to sneak up on him."

I took a pencil and the pad of paper I use for grocery lists from the kitchen, slipped out the back door and through the grad student's yard so I could cross the street behind the parked van.

The wind was up, humid and promising rain. The early spring leaves were just starting to come out, giving the trees a new sound. Soon the birds would be nesting, another Michigan spring. The street light down by the intersection was too distant to provide much light in the middle of our long block.

I sneaked up behind the van and turned my flashlight on the license plate. Illinois. I put the light down on the pavement while I started to write down the number.

The van engine started up with a roar, catching me on the last two digits of the number. Maybe my presence would drive them out of the neighborhood.

I wasn't prepared for them to put the transmission in reverse. The van lurched backwards. Caught in a crouch I barely had time to fling myself into the middle of the street. It was a glancing blow, but I was knocked down.

Now the van drove forward, peeling rubber down to the cul de sac turn-around at the end of the block. They made the turn, then came back.

I was so engrossed in what was happening that I didn't get out of the way. I realized that, standing there, I was silhouetted against the distant street light. Almost too late, I realized that the van was headed right toward me.

I jumped toward the curb just in time. Jackie Chan, eat your heart out.

The van lurched as it crunched over something, then roared away.

Stunned, I looked for the flashlight. It was crushed. I had dropped the pad of paper and had to grope for it in the dark.

Our front door opened, revealing Deborah, alarmed. "Adam? Are you all right?"

I found the pad with the license number, but the flashlight was a total loss. Shaken, I picked up the pieces and carried them over to show her. "See? This could have been me. Now who's paranoid?"

"Did you get the number?"

"Yes. Illinois plate. What are they doing here?"

"No telling. Could be someone thinking about home invasion. Maybe we should have a burglar alarm installed."

I remembered the door at Sarah's place in LA. "Or maybe one of those security screens."

"This is a split level house, not a fortress," Deborah said, hustling me inside. "Don't ask for bars on the windows. I don't want to live in a prison."

It was a close call, as they say. At least I did get a license number. "One thing we can do," I said. "That's report it as a hit and run personal injury accident. Then the police will look for the vehicle."

"Are you injured?"

I rubbed my shoulder. I was OK, just rattled. "Nothing that an insurance shyster can't pump up to a major claim for pain and suffering."

I called the Lansing police, but since I didn't need hospitalization, they wouldn't come out. I gave them a description of the van and the license number. I had no clue of its make or model. They promised to send me a report I could fill out. So much for law enforcement. This was beginning to look like Los Angeles. If it wasn't an out and out hostage shoot-out situation that attracted the news helicopters, why bother?

That more or less settled, Deborah poured me a nightcap and we calmed down with the Lansing State Journal-- the comics for me and the sports section for her-- and turned on the television.

We don't care much for the local newscasters and watch WGN out of Chicago. I thought I'd had enough excitement for one day, but there was more coming.

30.

I like the WGN TV news broadcast. Though I never lived there, it was my grandparents' territory and my cousins Jake and Miriam lived nearby. Grandpa and grandma Gold are buried side by side out in the old Waldheim Jewish cemetery with the Wobblies, victims or heroes of the famous Haymarket riot. I haven't been out there in years.

Pictures of the loop always remind me of Grandpa Abe Gold's news stand. I sometimes expect to see cousin Jake in those pictures of street mayhem, or Jake coming out of a courthouse with his coat over his face after an arraignment. Nothing like being related to celebrities.

Turns out it wasn't Jake that got the allotted fifteen minutes of fame or, more accurately for the eleven o'clock news, sixty seconds. The talking head said, "Police are searching for the killer or killers who brutally murdered another cab driver. Miriam Jakobi was shot three times. The motive appears to have been robbery. The robber or robbers got away with twenty-four dollars. This is the third killing of a cab driver in the last two months."

Could it be my cousin? I was horrified.

Sure enough. They put up a photograph of cousin Miriam, probably the one off her cabby's license. It was a straight ahead mug shot, penciled in eyebrows and all. It was only on for a moment before the cameras switched to a spokesman for the cabby's union.

The spokesperson was another female driver, a rough-looking woman about fifty with a face that had seen everything. With a wool watch cap she looked more like a stevedore than a cab driver. In a distinct Chicago accent, she said, "We gotta have more protection. Each cab has a plastic shield between the driver and the passengers, but Miriam Jakobi was shot like the others, through the back of the driver's seat with a powerful hand gun."

I couldn't help imagining the thunder of three pistol shots through the back of the driver's seart, tearing Miriam apart. My God. All that for twenty-four dollars?

Cut to the WGN announcer. "Driving a taxi is statistically the most dangerous job in the country, even more dangerous than being a policeman or fireman. Police are looking for anyone who might have witnessed Miriam Jakobi's murder." A number to call was flashed on the screen. "Cab drivers are planning a demonstration by blocking the Dan Ryan expressway tomorrow."

That would be a nice gesture of solidary for my cousin Miriam, but I didn't think the public would take notice. The Dan Ryan is always blocked.

Shaken, I told Deborah, "You can't tell me this one was an accident, too."

Deborah made an effort to reassure me. "A coincidence, Adam. It has to be a coincidence."

"Someone trying to run me over on the street was a coincidence, too, was it?"

"Maybe your prowling behind a couple of smoochers made the driver nervous and he put it in reverse by accident."

I wasn't buying it. I did a quick count. "Now there are only four of us: Schmuel, Jake, me and Harold."

"You're assuming Arthur is dead," Deborah said.

"As good as." I wasn't going to phone Cecile again to ask her if she'd pulled the plug on Arthur's life support. I felt a twinge of responsibility. What if I had gone to see him immediately instead of putting him off until Saturday? Would that have made any difference?

If Cecile pulled the plug on Arthur brother and sister might be buried at the same time. Such a deal. Two for the price of one. I couldn't stand it.

"I wonder if Cecile knows her sister-in-law has been murdered," I said.

"Don't you go calling her," Deborah cautioned. "She's got enough on her head."

"I suppose we'll get a call from Miriam's husband. Jeez, I can't even remember his name. I don't think I've ever met him."

"Just you wait. Don't meddle in their affairs, Adam. It's not your business."

"If it has anything to do with Aunt Sadie's tontine, it is my business, and yours. We could be next."

Deborah remembered that old Tonto and the Lone Ranger joke. Surrounded by wild Indians, the Lone Ranger says, "Looks like we've had it, Tonto." Deborah adopted the line, "What do you mean, 'we' white man?"

"Don't be funny," I said. "Funny doesn't make it go away."

Deborah put a comforting arm around my shoulder. "Adam, you can at least give me credit for trying."

Cousin Miriam's sixty seconds of fame was over. WGN was on the weather. Then would come sports.

I reached for the remote to shut it off and saw that my hands were shaking. It was too much. Sarah, Millie, Arthur, now Miriam, almost me with that van. The Lansing police should have no trouble tracing the owner, but would they tell me who it was?

I wondered, did Jake own a van? Maybe he had one for delivering newspapers. If Jake put a hit on me it would probably happen in the grocery store parking lot as I got out of the car. That's how the pros did it. Pop, pop, two quick shots to the head with a palm-size Beretta. I would have to add an item to my grocery list: remember to duck.

31.

The Lansing police did a better job than I expected. Someone called the next morning after Deborah left for the office. The license plate, it turned out, was stolen. That ruled out a smoocher accidentally shifting into reverse but it didn't lead us to the van or its driver. Another dead end. Maybe it was a good thing I was a house spouse and not a detective. I had trouble enough detecting dust mice under the bed.

Deborah called me from the office with a request. If I made a grocery run would I pick up her dry cleaning? Taking early retirement meant I was in the Honey do mode, "Honey do this, Honey, do that." Why not? Picking up the dry cleaning would give me a sense of importance. I could add that to the job description on my proposed business card.

Before I could report on the stolen license plate Deborah hung up. I decided not to call her back. No need for her to worry about our own when she had a client's troubles to sort out.

I finished the morning chores, swept the deck out back, grabbed my grocery list. The number of the purloined Illinois plate was on the top sheet. I crossed it out, scribbled in a couple of items, put on my jacket and went into the garage where the old Volvo was parked over its accumulation of oil drips.

Deborah had left the garage door open when she left for the office. I guess since I was home she didn't think it necessary to close it. You'd have thought that with the business of the van she'd have been more careful.

The Volvo wouldn't start. Not even a grunt. I knew I should have replaced that battery.

I used to recharge the battery from time to time by borrowing my neighbor's charger, but he had sold the house and that grad student lived there now, a renter with a female roommate. She didn't look like the type of girl who owned a battery charger.

I called Triple A. They'd send a truck, give me a jump start, and I'd drive to Sears for a new battery. One more stop for my list.

The wrecker arrived in twenty minutes, a monster of a vehicle. The fixture for flashing yellow lights on the roof barely cleared the garage portal as the wrecker pulled into Deborah's empty space beside the Volvo.

The guy from Triple A was an old geezer who had done this thousands of times. He looked to be over seventy, but as long as he could wrestle a tow bar into place and get under someone's axles to hook on chains, he could keep supplementing that social security. The name embroidered on his greasy blue coveralls was Fred.

I popped the hood and raised it for him as he came around with the heavy duty jumper cables. He was about to clamp them to the battery when he stopped.

"What's this?"

"What's what? Fred, don't tell me I only had a loose connection." I should have checked that myself.

"Don't touch anything," he warned me as he got a flashlight out of the cab of his truck. When he came back he trained the light on something under the hood.

My knees buckled when I saw what he was pointing at. No, no prankster had put a dead skunk on the manifold. I remembered all those action movies where the mobster gets into his car and it explodes in a roar of flame, pieces flying in all directions. Blowing up another Cadillac was just another item in the budget for a mobster movie. Blowing up an old Volvo was not in mine.

I had gassed up the car before driving to the airport for my flight to LA and the tank was still amost full. That would make a fire big enough and hot enough to leave nothing but the fillings in my teeth, if they could be found in the rubble of the house. If the battery had not been dead, that would have been my fate. I had a sudden need to go to the bathroom.

In the movies James Bond hesitates as the timer counts down to zero. "Don't cut the red wire," I warned.

"Lucky your battery is dead," Fred said, as he hastily packed the jumper cables back in his truck. "I ain't cutting any wire. You better call the cops."

I had a hard time explaining myself to the Lansing police, I was so rattled. They do respond to the word bomb. They came immediately. In fact, two police cars came screaming up the street to the house, blue lights flashing. I guess the second one was having a dull morning and wanted to get in on the excitement. In a minute I was surrounded by kids in blue uniforms. They looked at the device under the hood of my poor old Volvo, confirmed what Fred had identified and called for a backup.

"What are you going to do?" I asked. "I've never had anybody put a bomb in my car before."

The senior officer smiled facetiously. "It's not generally something you experience twice. We'll have to tow it to an open field someplace and set if off."

I noticed the senior officer had a name tag over his badge. Finelli. First names for menials like Fred, last names for people who commanded respect, like the police. "Wha-at? You're going to blow up my car? It's good for another hundred thousand miles."

"We'll have an expert check it out. If we can remove the device, you'll get your car back, though I can't see why you'd want it. What is it, fifteen years old?"

"Seventeen. In three more years I can get antique plates for it."

"But then you'll only be able to drive it in parades and rallies," Officer Finelli explained. "Now why don't we go sit in the patrol car at a safe distance? You can explain to me why someone would put a bomb in your car. You involved in something illegal, Mr. Rottman? Like drugs? You wouldn't be dealing cocaine, would you?"

The way he said it made me feel guilty. I guess he expected a confession. I didn't oblige. We got into the patrol car and Officer Finelli moved it to a safe distance, the same spot where the van had nearly run me over.

It was hard to concentrate on my story, for I kept watching the police to see what they were doing inside my garage. I had visions of the car exploding and the whole house going up in flames.

"I think it's the tontine," I said.

"What's a tontine?"

I explained Aunt Sadie's estate, that my sister Sarah got the proceeds while she was alive, and that if she didn't turn up, she being missing, the last survivor of the cousins would get the whole caboodle, the caboodle being a reported one million dollars.

"Sounds like you have some impatient relatives," Finelli said. He was writing down every word in his little book.

"You might have seen that I reported a hit and run attempt on my life yesterday," I said. "I got the tag number but the plate turned out to be stolen. Probably the people in that van were checking to see what our habits were, when my wife went to work, stuff like that, so they'd know when they could come in and put the bomb in my car. It wouldn't do to put it in my wife's. Deborah's not on the list. She can't inherit Sadie's money."

"You have a burglar alarm in your house?"

"No."

"Better get one installed. I'm not guaranteeing if someone wants to kill you that we'll get there in time to save your life, Mr. Rottman, but we might be in time to catch whoever does. They've apparently tried twice. Three strikes and you're out."

I told him Millie had been run over by a car, Arthur had been fire bombed and Miriam shot dead in her taxi. Finelli's job was to be suspicious of everyone. "And you weren't anywhere near them, so you have a solid alibi."

"Of course."

"And you didn't put the bomb in your car yourself to throw suspicion on someone else?"

"I don't know anything about explosives. I don't even set off fire crackers on the Fourth of July."

"Do you own a firearm, Mr. Rottman? In your circumstances, you could probably get a permit to carry a concealed weapon. That's what I'd do."

"I've never fired a gun of any kind, officer. I'm afraid of them."

Finelli shook his head. "It's your funeral."

"Don't talk about funerals," I said. "I just attended two and there's at least one more coming-- if I go."

"For your cousin, the taxi driver?"

"Yes, Miriam. I hadn't planned on it. I hardly knew her."

"With all this tontine business, I'm sure the Chicago police will have detectives at the funeral to see who shows up. It might be a good idea for you to be there, Mr. Rottman."

"Why? Just to show the killer I'm still alive? To give him another chance?"

Finelli nodded. "You'll be surrounded by detectives. If someone did make an attempt on your life at the funeral, you'd have some protection."

"Jake's the only one capable of any of this," I said.

"Jake?"

I didn't want to say too much about Jake and his business. All I had was hearsay, anyway, family rumors. "Family rumor has it that Jake's a bookie or something." I didn't want to say that my brother called Jake Mafia Man.

"Some family," Finelli said. "Anybody else I should know about?"

"Cousin Schmuel's in Los Angeles. He's a jerk. I can't imagine my brother Harold being involved."

Officer Finelli shook his head. "Families. What would the police do without them?"

Considering the craziness in mine, I wondered if I'd have been better off as an orphan.

32.

Even though I was reasonably certain that whoever rigged my car was after me and not Deborah, I couldn't take any chances and not warn her. I broke her rule and phoned her at the office. When she picked up I said, "Do you have a client?"

"A client is coming in in five minutes. What's up, Adam?" She sounded irritated.

"The license plate on the van was stolen. They can't trace the car."

"That figures." She sensed the urgency in my voice. "Something else. What?"

I didn't know where to begin. "I won't be able to pick up the dry cleaning."

"You called me at the office for that?" Now she was getting cross.

"No. Wait. Before you start your car, look under the hood and make sure nobody put a bomb on the engine."

"Adam!" she said sharply. "What did I tell you about your paranoid fantasies?"

"The police were just here. The Volvo wouldn't start, Boruch Hashem. Imagine me thanking God that my car won't start? When the triple A guy went to put on the jumper cables he found a bomb under the hood. You forgot to close the garage door and they got inside and put a bomb in my car."

There was silence for a long moment. When Deborah spoke again, her tone had become very professional. "What did the police do with your car?"

"They towed it away. They might blow it up. I'm hoping they'll just remove the device and check it for fingerprints. My guess is that there won't be any. It was a very neat package, from what I could see of it. Someone who had practice, had done it before."

"What did the police say you should do?"

"Officer Finelli told me to go to Miriam's funeral and to notify the Chicago police so they'll have detectives there in case whoever shot her shows up. I don't even know when or where the funeral will be."

"I'm not letting you go alone," Deborah said.

"Good. Maybe on the way to it, wherever it is, we could do a little shopping. Pick up a couple of bullet proof vests."

"Very funny, Adam."

"Not funny, not funny. Serious."

"Any word from Cecile?"

"I'll call her, too."

"And call your sweet brother Harold. I'll bet he'll be satisfied."

"Satisfied? Why should Harold be satisfied?"

She didn't answer that one. "My client's here. Got to go. Sit tight until I get home."

"So what else would I do?" I began, and would have said, "I can't drive anywhere and after what happened to Millie I'm afraid to cross the street," but she had hung up.

I couldn't find my address book with Miriam's phone number at first, and when I did the number I had scribbled in God knows how many years ago had been changed. The new number rang a long time before someone picked it up, a young male voice.

"Is this the Jakobi's residence?" I asked.

"Yeh, who's this?"

"Adam Rottman. Miriam's cousin in Lansing, Michigan. We heard the news on the TV last night. I'm terribly shocked. Who am I talking to?"

It was her son, Ira, home from college on short notice. He told me that the funeral arrangements hadn't been made yet because they had to get the body back from the postmortem. They hadn't made any arrangements. Here Ira's voice choked up and he couldn't continue.

I couldn't either, even to offer condolances. I imagined Miriam's corpse laid out naked on a slab for the police photographer's evidence file. She hadn't been a pretty woman, but there was something immodest and invasive about being laid out like that naked for strangers to examine. They'd probably have to check, too, to see if she was raped, swab her vagina for semen and DNA testing, stuff like that. Routine for the coroner. My cousin Miriam would be just another corpse to them.

I wondered what kind of an exit wound you got if someone shot you in the back through the seat of a taxi. Did the bullets make big, gaping holes, or did they stay inside the body, part of their terrible energy absorbed by the foam upholstery?

I pulled myself out of those horrible images. "This is awful, Ira. I'll see if I can find you some help." I gave Ira my number and insisted that he repeat it and write it down. He was in no state to remember anything.

Help? Where would I go for help in Chicago? I had put things off long enough. It was time to call Jake.

I had wanted to see him face to face when I told him about Arthur and the fire and decided not to mention that for now. If I could confine the conversation to just Miriam's funeral I could keep things safe and neutral. Thank you, Deborah, for all that coaching on interpersonal relationships. Those courses in psychology had some value after all.

I was in luck. The number I had for Jake was current. Jake was organized. I could tell by the rings that he had call forwarding. When he answered, the traffic sounds in the background told me he had a cell phone. He was probably downtown at his news stand. "Yeh? Who's this?"

"Your cousin Adam, Adam Rottman."

"Really?" Jake sounded surprised.

Maybe he expected me to be dead already. I didn't go there, but instead asked if he had heard about Miriam being shot.

"Yeh," Jake said, not surprised at that. "These punks. They'll kill you for nothing. What did they get? They said on the news twenty-four dollars. Imagine bumping off a cabby for a lousy twenty-four bucks?"

I didn't say that maybe they got paid bigger money up front and the twenty four dollars was just to make it look like a robbery. "Miriam's son Ira says they haven't made any arrangements about a funeral or anything. Where would she be buried?"

Jake was, indeed, organized. "Since you mention it, Miriam can have Aunt Sadie's plot. Originally Sadie was supposed to be buried in the family plot out at Waldheim cemetery. There's two vacant graves next to great grandpa Isaac, grandpa Abe and grandma."

So, I thought, when Arthur dies they can have a family reunion. Considering the horror of driving through Chicago I almost wished they'd both be buried at once to save an extra trip.

Of course, if the bomb had gone off in my car, it might be me making the trip to Waldheim, but I wouldn't be driving myself, not from a box in the back of a hearse.

I decided not to tell Jake about the bomb in my car. For all I knew, Jake had ordered that little present on my behalf and it wasn't even my birthday. "Will you call the Jakobis and offer the cemetery plot? Have someone let me know when the funeral will be. I do want to be there. Family support and all that."

"That's nice of you, Adam. It would be a mitzvah."

A mitzvah, a good deed. What did Jake know from good deeds? On the other hand, if he offered a cemetery plot for Miriam, that was a mitzvah. Maybe I had misjudged Jake.

I didn't have the energy left to call Cecile to find out Arthur's condition. I didn't want to talk to Harold, either. I'd had enough for one day.

What I needed was something to take my mind off all this stuff. Maybe I'd bake a cake. There's nothing like focusing on a simple task like pushing a spoon around a mixing bowl to take your mind off other things. We had a bunt cake mix in the cupboard and some rum left from my last effort. I'd make a rum cake. Deborah would like that.

When I preheated the oven something inside startd to smoke. For a terrifying moment I thought someone had booby trapped my oven so when I fired it up I'd be incinerated, like Arthur. If someone wanted you dead, there were lots of ways to do it. If someone wanted me scared silly, it was working.

33.

By the time Deborah came home from the office she had thought it all out. She's such a rational person. She came in the door, dropped her briefcase, gave me a reassuring embrace and a long kiss, then sniffed. "You've been baking."

"Rum cake," I said. Some spouses conquer the world. I do a little cooking.

"Nice," she said, then surprised me by pouring herself a shot of Bailey's Irish Creme. She never does that. "We have to talk." She sank into her eight hundred dollar leather chair and sighed, sipped her Bailey's, savoring the taste. Then she set her drink on the end table, careful to put in on the coaster I'd left there. "This tontine business. You realize it's all Harold's fault."

"Why is that? He said the tontine was Sadie's idea."

"Don't be naive, Adam. Sadie was an old woman, over ninety. You think your slick brother Harold couldn't talk her out of anything, or into it, for that matter?"

"I didn't know Sadie well enough to say one way or another," I admitted.

"In any case, it's done now," Deborah said. "The wolves are out of the pen."

"What do you mean?"

"Adam, if someone wants to kill you, they will. If they don't run you over or blow you up..."

I finished her sentence for her. "Or pop me in the back of the head in the grocery store parking lot, or outside Murray's steak house.

"Right. Or in some public bathroom when you go in to take a pee. You read about it all the time."

I was getting dry mouth. My hands were shaking. I rarely have a happy hour drink. Wine is more my speed, but we keep liquor in the place mostly for guests. Bailey's Irish Creme struck me as too sweet and cloying for my thirst so I fetched a cold Fresca from the fridge and popped the can. I had to clutch it with both hands to hold it steady. "So what do we do?"

"I'm not sure what we can do. You said the bomb was done by a professional. Miriam's death could have been done so it looked like a simple robbery of a taxi driver. Arthur's fire was no accident. I don't think any of your precious cousins committed those acts themselves. I think they hired them out."

"So what do we do?"

"I'm getting to that. Adam, you realize it could be any of your relatives, and it could be more than one. One million dollars is a lot of money. If, just for discussion purposes, Schmuel hired someone to torch Arthur and Jake put a hit on Miriam, now that they're out of the way, they might order hits on each other and Harold, and you. Once this kind of thing gets rolling, it can be hard to stop. If, just for instance, Schmuel ordered a hit on you but Jake's boys kill him first, then it's too late for Schmuel to cancel a contract for your murder. Right?"

"Oh, brother." I sat down on the couch, feeling helpless and surrounded.

"If your sister Sarah was the type, and I don't know her that well, she could be hiding out somewhere and ordering these killings herself, just as insurance that the Golds don't go after her first to open up the route to the money."

I thought of my silly sister with her Raggedy Ann and Andy doll collection. "I can't believe she'd do that."

"But Harold could, just to protect her."

I thought of Harold, his three hundred pound bulk wheezing at his Naptown law office desk, plotting that kind of protection for Sarah. He'd set up the trust so she'd get the proceeds. He could have made more deadly arrangements. "I don't know who to trust, Deborah. My God, what'll we do?"

"You can trust me, Adam. You can be sure I'm going to do what I can to see that you're the last survivor."

"Gee, thanks." It was a flat statement.

Deborah savored the taste of the last of her drink and winked. "After all, Adam, it's you who can inherit the million dollars, not me."

She meant it as a joke to cheer me up, but it shocked me that she could have thoughts like that. She's not even a Gold. "I don't care about Sadie's money. I just want to survive. So what are we going to do?"

"We've got to persuade the Golds that are left that Sarah is alive and that anything that jeopardizes her kills their chances of inheritance." Then she added, "And if they've already contracted for a hit on any of the remaining cousins, they should call it off."

"How do we do that?"

"I don't know yet," she admitted, "but I'm thinking."

"What if we concocted a story that Sarah was found, that she's alive and well and if she dies under mysterious circumstances Sadie's money goes to charity?"

Deborah looked at me over the tops of her glasses. "Adam, you're such an awful liar. I don't think you could persuade anybody."

She was right. Maybe that's why Harold always kept me in the dark when he was hatching his nefarious schemes. Harold and I had not been close. I was beginning to understand why.

34.

The Lansing police bomb expert managed to remove the device without blowing up my vintage Volvo, but they didn't return the car. By some error or malice they impounded it. This time it was my own car and not Sarah's drowned Volkswagen I had to bail out. They charged me a towing fee and two day's storage even though it was only there overnight! Talk about chutzpah. Time to write a complaint to the City Council.

When I did get the car paid for, it wouldn't start and again I had to call Triple A. The vehicle that drove through the gate of the Lansing impoundment lot was familiar, and the mechanic, too, Fred of the greasy blue coveralls and seventy-year-old wrinkly face. "No bomb this time?" Fred asked, not entirely sure. He was smoking.

"The police got rid of that."

"That's nice," he said as he dug the heavy jumper cables out of their stowage compartment.

"Keep up those cigarettes and you'll never make it to ninety," I cautioned.

Fred didn't say anything, but he did grind the butt out on the sole of his boot. He got to work on the Volvo.

It looked like the police had removed the inside door panels and more or less disassembled the Volvo in case, as Finelli had suggested, I really was dealing cocaine or some other controlled substance. I told Fred, "Once we get it started I'll drive to Sears for a new battery." Which I did.

Fred was considerate enough to follow me in the wrecker all the way to Sears just in case the Volvo stalled at a traffic light and had to be jumped again.

With a new battery the Volvo started up like a nervous filly out of the box on race day but it didn't handle the same as before. It didn't seem like the same car, like it had been violated. Driving it was in some way similar to having sex with someone who had recently been raped. It just wasn't the same. Maybe I had driven that heap for too long and it was time to trade it in. I would never feel the same about it again when I hit the starter. I would fear an explosion, the concussion and flames of instant death. That is, assuming you have time to feel instant death.

On the way back from Sears I remembered the dry cleaning, dutiful house spouse than I am, and picked it up. I'll do anything to satisfy my wife, though I can think of some better ways than by picking up a power business suit at the cleaners.

Then it was back to the phones: first Cecile. Arthur had told me a life without risk wasn't much of a life. Trouble is, sometimes when you take a risk you lose. The doctors said Arthur wasn't responding. His lungs were badly damaged by smoke. If he did come out of a coma he would have to schlep an oxygen tank around with him the rest of his life.

Cecile didn't look to me like the kind of person who wanted to be caregiver for someone that disabled, but you never can tell. Some people have depths of reserve strength and courage you wouldn't suspect.

Cecile explained, "If he doesn't show any sign of brain activity in another twenty-four hours, the doctors and I are going to have a meeting." Her voice was matter of fact. She'd thought about this a lot. What will I do if? What's the next step after that?

I'd guess she was already wondering what she'd wear for the funeral. Was that how women thought? Or was it my Gold chromosome acting up.

I didn't want to force that conclusion. "What do you think the outcome of your meeting with the doctors will be?"

"We'll turn off life support."

Grim thought, the person you love still breathing, all those tubes and wires, the respirator's rhythmic hissing, and you decide to end it. Almost like murder. "If they pull the plug, how long can he live?"

Cecile sounded resigned. "I don't know. Minutes, maybe hours. That's what I hope the doctors will tell me."

I changed the subject to Miriam. "Did you hear about Miriam? Shot to death in her taxi? It was on the WGN news. The cabbies are staging a protest demonstration on the Dan Ryan expressway. I think it's today."

Cecile hadn't heard about the death of her sister-in-law and was suitably shocked. She exclaimed, "Oh, my God, oh my God," and sounded like she was losing it altogether until I got her attention. Speaking slowly to try to calm her down I explained what Jake had said about the two vacant cemetery plots, that Arthur could have one of them, if it came to that. I emphasized the "if" on the assumption if Arthur had any hope of recovery Cecile might feel better. We both knew he didn't.

Sometimes if you focus on other details you can take your mind off what's upsetting you. I didn't know where the funerals would take place. I envisioned a long line of mourners' cars with their little magnetic funeral flag and headlights on as they proceeded to the cemetery. It would take some coordination, but brother and sister could be laid to rest at the same time. I wasn't being selfish, about the driving and that. It just seemed fitting to me that brother and sister could be buried together.

I also explained about the police, what Finelli had said about the killer or killers possibly showing up. Detectives would probably be checking the guest books and taking down license numbers of all the cars.

There's a time in life when you go to a lot of graduation parties, another time for weddings, brises and naming ceremonies, annual reunions and finally for funerals. I had gone to a lot of funerals lately. My whole family was dying off in quick succession.

Hell, my brother Harold could croak any time from emphysema or a heart attack. Jake could be whacked by one of his underworld competitors. Schmuel could be nagged to death. Or, as Deborah had put it, we could all be bumped off by contract killers. I had already had two close calls and was hoping not another.

In case she didn't already have it, I gave Cecile Jake's phone number and the Jakobis'. Once arrangements were made she should call me so Deborah and I could be at the funerals.

I was looking up Harold's number at his law office when the phone rang right under my hand. I jumped like I'd been bitten and dropped the receiver on the floor. I picked it up. "Yes?"

The voice was young and eager. "This is Sue Nelson, reporter for the Lansing State Journal. We got a tip that your car was bombed. What's the story?"

Jesus, where did they find that out? "Somebody must be leaking misinformation at the police department," I said. "There's no story. My car was not bombed." This was supposed to be confidential so the police could do their investigation without public fanfare. "Who told you my car was blown up?" It was a sneaky diversion. She had said bombed, I said blown up. It had been bombed in the sense that a bomb had been put in it. I didn't want to admit that.

Now Sue Nelson-- I hastily scribbled down her name so I'd remember-- got defensive. "We don't reveal our sources of information."

"Then I respectfully suggest that you find some other 'authoritative' source, someone reliable. My car is quite intact. You can see for yourself."

Who could have blabbed about the bomb? Officer Finelli would keep his mouth shut, but one of the rookies who swarmed around my car might not be as discreet. Sue Nelson might have a scanner, but the cops used codes to keep their radio transmissions secure. Would Sue Nelson know the police code for car bomb?

What about Fred? Triple A wouldn't have a code of silence. Maybe telling the story of the attempt on my life gave Fred his sound bite in front of a TV camera, his one moment of fame.

I wanted no such fame. Anonymity. That was my goal in all this. I did not want to be seen or noticed.

Sue Nelson apologized for the inconvenience, but she didn't sound convinced. As a reporter, deny, deny, deny was a tactic she had to be familiar with. If she didn't get her story from me, she might try someone else.

I prayed for a tornado or something catastrophic that would grab the front page, pushing mere car bombs out of the public eye. Maybe Iran could declare war on Brazil or something. Then Sue Nelson wouldn't bother me. She'd be off in her foreign correspondent field jacket for the Big Story. Anything but mine.

At least for now she wouldn't bother me. Before I hung up I promised her, "If my car is blown up I'll try to let you know in advance so your photographer can get a nice picture. You'll have to compete with the television station, though. You know how they like those action shots."

I still had one call to make: Harold. A cab driver shooting in Chicago was not news in Naptown as we used to call Indianapolis. It wouldn't be reported there. Naptown would have their own corpses to report on.

Somehow, Harold knew about Miriam. Bad news travels fast. Maybe Deborah was right: he'd ordered the killing himself. I couldn't believe that of my own brother, but the way things were developing I was losing trust in everyone.

I explained that Jake could arrange burial plots for both Arthur and Miriam in the old Waldheim cemetery. This time Harold would have to be there. I insisted.

"I don't like funerals," Harold said, wheezing. "They remind me of my own."

"Then you'll just have to deal with it. Will you drive up or fly?"

"I hadn't thought about it," Harold said, putting me off.

"The police will probably be among the crowd, looking for whoever torched the Gents' club or shot Miriam." For a fleeting moment I imagined a shoot-out at the graveyard, the surviving Golds taking pot shots at one another, the plain clothes cops getting into the fray, and extra bodies dropping into the open graves like in a bad movie.

"They won't be there," Harold said. It sounded like he knew for sure. What else did he know that he wasn't telling me?

"Why not?"

Harold paused, weighing his words again in true judicial style. "If both of these alleged incidents were done by professionals, whoever did them has no personal interest in the victims or in any of us. All people like that care about is the money. They take their pay, do the deed, and skip.

"How do you know all this?" I asked.

"I once represented a professional hit man who managed to blunder and get caught. You'd be surprised at the extent of that kind of thing."

"Really?" Maybe Harold had got someone off who owed him a favor in lieu of legal fees. "How do you know that?"

"I just know."

Maybe it was common knowledge that I in my naive ignorance was unaware of. "Maybe Murder Incorporated is a dot com organization with a web page."

Harold agreed. "I wouldn't be surprised at anything, Adam."

"Would you be surprised if I told you someone put a bomb in my car? The only reason it didn't go off was because the battery was dead." I told him the story. He sounded disturbed, but not surprised.

"You should be careful yourself, Harold. Someone might put a bomb in your Cadillac. How do you order a car bombing?"

"You could look it up," Harold said, being sarcastic. "Try the internet. You might very well solve this from your home computer."

As it turned out, he was right, but that was still a long way off.

As for attending two funerals in one day and a joint burial, Harold refused to make a commitment.

I didn't call Schmuel. If anything, he'd probably gloat over the removal of two more names from the tontine list. At the best of times I couldn't stand his asinine attitude and these were definitely not the best of times.

As for the internet, that was an intriguing idea. I wondered if Murder Incorporated really was a dot com organization. If you could get phone sex, buy dildos, and X-rated videos off the World Wide Web, why not do a contract for murder? It might seem absurd, but absurd was much more comfortable than thinking that Harold had such connections and might use them.

35.

As Cecile had expected, the doctors pulled the plug on Arthur. Unable to breathe on his own, he was dead in a few minutes. As I suggested, she coordinated with the Jakobis. Arthur's funeral would be at a mortician's in Hobart in the morning and Miriam's would be in the Waldheim chapel in the afternoon. The bodies would both be brought from there to the cemetery in one combined procession.

It would be a long, momentous day.

Pro forma, Schmuel and Sylvia had been advised-- not by me-- that two more of the cousins were dead. Though Arthur and Miriam had cared enough to make it to LA for Millie's funeral, I didn't expect Schmuel to fly to Chicago for Arthur and Miriam's. Schmuel didn't seem to me to be the caring type. Besides, if he was as broke as Sylvia claimed, they'd have to find a credit card that wasn't topped out to get the plane tickets, even at the compassionate rate airlines offer for mourners.

I had no idea who would show up or what arrangements might be done with the police. I called Officer Finelli to find out what coordination, if any, was made with the Chicago police. I visualized faxes flying back and forth. Taken separately, there would have been no obvious connection between Sarah's disappearance, Millie's traffic accident, Arthur's fire and Miriam's armed robbery and shooting. With the tontine to connect them this was taking on the character of a Hatfields and McCoys family feud or, just as brutal, a gang war. I was reminded of the Alec Guinness movie, "Kind Hearts and Coronets," in which an an ambitious relative seven inheritors removed from a royal title does them all in. The difference was, that was a movie, a black comedy. This was real and it was potentially every man for himself out to get all the others. Except me. I wasn't out to get anyone. When someone puts a bomb in your own car, it might be a black one, but it's not a comedy.

Finelli wouldn't give out any information. He still suspected me. If I had conveniently "discovered" my own bomb just to throw any investigators off the track, they weren't going to tell me who or how many police would be at the funerals of Arthur and Miriam or at the cemetery. It was further complicated because Arthur was in Indiana and Miriam in Illinois. Indiana cops weren't likely to go to a Chicago funeral and vice versa. Was Finelli, a Lansing, Michigan policeman, going to Chicago to follow up on the aborted bombing of my Volvo? Hardly. That's where criminals had the edge. They didn't respect state lines, but the local police had no jurisdiction outside their own territory and had to rely on cooperation. No wonder Calumet City dives like Arthur's Gents' Club thrived.

Would Finelli tell the Chicago police that I was a suspect? I didn't mind. I knew I was innocent, and if they thought I wasn't and put a tail on me I saw it as protection. A police presence would be welcome. I'd be happy if it was the police parked across the street instead of that mysterious van. I could use a couple of guardian angels.

On the other hand, the scandals in the Chicago police department suggested that they might be so eager to solve a case that they'd arrest anyone and fake the evidence. Hadn't half the men on death row been exonerated when it was found-- thanks to a Northwestern University professor and his students who investigated-- that the police had done that? The Illinois courts were too eager to impose the death penalty. The worst case scenario was that the Chicago cops would make up a story, charge me with contracting for Miriam's death to get Sadie's money, and put me in the slammer. There was no guarantee some Northwestern University professor would put his students on my case and get me out. I would have to be careful not to spit on the sidewalk or jaywalk while in Chicago.

Deborah was at her office downtown. At home I had laundry to do. I can make a single bath towel go for a couple of weeks, but Deborah, being a woman, has hair. The towels pile up. While the load ran, instead of just dusting her home computer I logged on to AOL. It's Deborah's account and you just click for the password to be entered automatically. Deborah trusts me. Just for the heck of it I tried Yahoo in search of Murder Incorporated dot com.

There were far too many sites that had something to do with murder. I had to do a more limited search. Since Murder

Incorporated had at one time been a real organization, there were stories and essays and old articles cross indexed to organized crime but no dot com. I tried searching for MurderIncorporated.com and Murder.Incorporated.com and Murder.inc.com but none of the variations worked.

I was now afraid that somewhere in the system there was a record of what I had searched for. What if the police asked AOL if I surfed in search of a contract killer? Good thing I had never used the computer to look for "How to Make a Car Bomb" information. Finelli would soon be on to that.

Deborah had put the Raggedy Ann doll that Sarah gave me on top of the bookcase in her home office. I wondered what the doll might be worth so logged on to E-bay, Sarah's marketplace for her collection.

I could see right away that shopping on E-bay could be addictive. It was an auction, the items up for sale up to a given moment at which time the deal was either closed or the item withdrawn for lack of interest.

When I found Raggedy Ann on E-bay I was astonished. Among the first fifty offered there were paper Raggedy Anns, nesting Russian Raggedies, dolls of cloth, hand made, big and little, rare, mint, patterns for dolls for the do-it-yourselfer, dolls in different costumes and a full range of prices from about three bucks to over a hundred. I had never guessed, even from Sarah's collection, that this was an international business attracting aficionados from all over the world. Who were all these doll collectors? And if I were to sell the doll Sarah pressed into my arms at the Los Angeles airport, how would I describe it and what was it worth? I hadn't a clue.

Maybe it was time I found out. The towels were washed, so went into the drier. While they dried I stayed logged on at the Raggedy Ann site, bookmarked it so I could get back to it quickly, and started working my way down the first fifty hits.

It was interesting. You had just so much time to make a bid and if you won you mailed a money order to the person and they sent you the merchandise. To reduce the likelihood of fraud, E-bay customers were encouraged to send in comments on the performance of the seller. Of course, you could have your cohorts send in fake laudatory statements about you, but anyone you cheated would soon spill the beans. Trust on E-bay was an elusive commodity to be nurtured, not sold.

Another peculiarity about the E-bay sellers and buyers was their anonymity. Everybody was identified by a code name. I made a list. Considering the product they were selling, the names were what you might expect: Raggy, a name so popular that there was a Raggy2, Raggy3, etc., Mamadoll, Dollbaby, Dolly, Andy, Andy2, and so on. The rule was, you didn't find out the real name of the person until you won a bid. That got you the name and address where to send the money order.

I studied the list while folding the laundry. I couldn't remember what Sarah's E-bay business name was. I'm not much for puzzles, never do crosswords. My mind seizes up like an engine without oil when I hit stumbling blocks like this. Remembering which clothes were washed warm and gentle and not hot with bleach was mental challenge enough for me.

If Sarah were not drowned in the Los Angeles drainage ditch, a.k.a. river, and still alive, hiding out in Acapulco she might be tempted, addict that she was, to do doll deals on E-bay. She could do that from anywhere, anywhere in the world.

Considering what Deborah had said about fooling the relatives into thinking Sarah was alive, I might be able to make up a credible lie that even I could tell without blushing.

That damned doll collection. If Sarah's body was never found, eventually someone in the family would have to dispose of her junk. Knowing how Harold operated, it was probably me. He thought just because I was retired and a house spouse meant I had nothing better to do. I bet Harold doesn't fold towels!

I did not look forward to the task of doing an inventory of Sarah's massive collection. How would I describe those dolls in such a way that someone reading the description would be able to distinguish one doll from any other? To me, when I first saw them, they all looked alike. It would not be easy.

I hadn't called Schmuel back to find out if he'd posted a missing person ad in the LA Times. With all the excitement about Miriam's shooting and the bomb in my car I hadn't gotten back to the LA Missing Persons office, either.

My call to the LA police yielded nothing. Sarah's body had not turned up. Considering some of the police cases I'd seen in the paper, it might be years before someone stumbled on a skeleton and the dental records identified my poor, dead sister. By then the tontine thing could have run its course, down to the last survivor.

I couldn't remember who I had talked to at the LA Times. Where had I written down that name?

You know how it is when you can't find something. You go crazy. I had dutifully tidied up. I finally found the Times notation on the back of an envelope under the phone in the living room. Liz Tompkins.

Liz Tompkins had forgotten all about my previous call. No, Schmuel had not delivered a photo for a story on my missing sister Sarah. It was clear that in LA a missing person was of no interest to anyone but that person's own family, or the person herself. To Liz Tompkins it was already old news which to a newspaper person is no news worth mentioning.

The next step would be the funerals of my cousins, but since we would be driving west again, this time I would take along the keys to the family cottage at the lake just in case we decided to have another look. Now let's see if I could find them.

Shouldn't be hard, I reasoned. I have a key board on the inside of our broom closet in the mud room. The door latch doesn't work properly. The keys are forever falling off the hooks when I slam the door shut. Then the next time I open the door there's a pile of keys on the floor. So much for my neat system of labeled hooks.

You wouldn't believe how many keys one accumulates over the years, luggage keys, desk keys, garage door, car, bicycle, padlock keys, the whole gamut. The locks may be long since deceased and discarded but I hang onto the keys in the remote hope that one day I'll need a key and viola! this old one will fit. They never have.

At least I keep them in one place. There are no keys-- not to my knowledge-- lurking in the bottom of my desk drawer, under Deborah's underwear, under the floor mat by the front door, or taped under the mail box.

Unfortunately, they don't all have tags. Some are just anonymous keys. I spread them all out on the washing machine lid and tried to eliminate them one by one. I wasn't going to schlep a bucket of keys when we drove to Arthur's and Miriam's funerals.

At last I settled on three probables, all tarnished brass cylinder lock door keys different from those I could identify with certainty. I put those in a manila envelope and started writing a list for when we went to the funerals. At the top of it: take keys.

Then I started making up a story about Sarah being alive and well in Mexico and doing doll deals on E-bay. I only wished it was true. Knowing it wasn't would make it difficult for me to bring the story off.

I would have to do it convincingly to get whoever it was that wanted me dead to call off the mad dogs. That meant I had to tell it to Schmuel the schmuck, Mafia man Jake, and even Harold. Would they believe me? If they didn't, I was as good as dead. But then, if more than one relative was into this murder thing, so were all the others.

The commandment was "Thou shalt not bear false witness," translated as "Thou shalt not lie." Lucky for me, in Judaism it is permissible to break any commandment if it means saving a life, like even eating pork if pork was the only antidote for cobra bites. Did that count if I was trying to save my own life? I hoped so.

36.

Deborah had to cancel all her clients for the day of the funeral. When she came home she was preoccupied and worried. I threw together a nice vegetarian stir fry with steamed rice and bamboo shoots which we ate in the kitchen. Deborah hardly spoke through the meal.

"Sorry I'm out of fortune cookies," I said. "I hope rum cake will do." That cheered her up.

"We'll probably have to stay overnight after the burials," she said. "It'll be too late in the day to drive back to Lansing."

"Maybe someone will invite us over," I said.

Deborah raised an eyebrow at that one. "You willing to stay overnight at Mafia Man Jake's if he offers?"

"You think he'll kill me in his own house?" I shuddered.

"Why not? Maybe he's got his mother-in-law buried in the basement. What's another relative more or less?"

I hoped she was kidding. Sometimes it's hard to tell. "We'll find a hotel and not tell anyone where we are."

We packed overnight bags and set them by the door to the garage so they'd be ready.

Arthur's funeral was to be in Hobart at ten in the morning and Miriam's in the afternoon. It would be tough, getting from one to the other through all that traffic and then to the cemetery before the grave diggers quit for the day. At least the time change would be in our favor. We'd pick up an hour crossing into Indiana.

I couldn't fall asleep. That list of all the doll sellers on E-bay nagged at me. Frustrated, not wanting to wake Deborah, I went to the kitchen and sat at the kitchen table studying the list of names. Raggy, Raggy2, Raggy3, Mamadoll, Mamadoll2, Dollbaby, Dolly, Andy, Andy2, Andy3, Doll1, Doll2. Could any of them be Sarah? How could I find out?

It was cold in the kitchen and I hadn't put on my slippers. Shivering, I moved though the living toom to Deborah's office. Millie's Shiva candle was still flickering on the mantlepiece. The sight of it put me in a funk. Now there would be another, at Cecilie's and Miriam's. Did they have mantlepieces, too? Where would they put their mourning candles?

Once in Deborah's office I turned on her computer. Computers are not my thing. I don't do e-mail, don't get daily jokes or surf the internet, though I've watched over Deborah's shoulders sometimes. I'm not a total computer illiterate nor one of those people who refuse to have one in the house, but I do admit to being intimidated. I suppose great grandpa Isaac would have felt the same way when he saw his first automobile. Except great grandpa Isaac would have quickly stolen it even if he didn't know how to drive.

Windows 98 came up and I logged on to Deborah's AOL account. I had bookmarked the Raggedy Ann site and it came right up. There they all were, the paper Raggedies, the nesting Russian Raggedies, the mint-condition-in-original-box Raggedy Andy, the miniature ones in porcelain. And the code names of the sellers.

How could I find out if one of the sellers on e-Bay was Sarah Rottman? And if it was Sarah, how could I get the current address? This was going to take time.

I figured, as I fumbled my way through the web site, that the only way I could find out the addresses of sellers was to win a bid on the dolls. What would I do if I won all the bids and ended up with a busted savings account and fifty dumb dolls? If I could only remember Sarah's pseudonym. When had I seen it?

I thought back to Sadie's Shiva event in Sarah's awful apartment. Standing by her computer at her kitchen table piled with doll paraphernalia Sarah had shown me how she made deals on e-Bay. "That's my offer," she had said, pointing to the screen. "Mamadoll. That's me."

Whoever called himself or herself Mamadoll now was offering a mint condition Raggedy Andy in a gingham outfit, twenty-seven inches high, asking for a five hundred dollar minimum bid. The current bid was five hundred and twenty. The bidding would close at noon tomorrow, or, rather, today, since it was already past two in the morning. Did these crazy collectors do doll deals twenty-four hours a day? Why didn't they speculate on some real commodity, like pork bellies?

Maybe it was because pork bellies didn't have shoe button eyes.

From what I understood of e-Bay, the only way I could find out if Mamadoll was Sarah was to win the bid. The only way to make a bid was to have an account, and I didn't have the first clue.

It had been quiet in the house, but now I heard a noise outside Deborah's office.

"What'cha doing?" It was Deborah in her nightgown and slippers. "Looking for pictures of naked women? How about this one?" She pulled up the front of her nightie.

"It's a bit early in the morning to flash me," I said. "I'm looking for Sarah."

"You're looking for Sarah on my computer? You better be careful. I have confidential client files on that."

"I'm not snooping your clients' sex lives. Sarah buys and sells dolls on e-Bay," I explained. "Her code name is Mamadoll. Someone named Mamadoll is auctioning off a Raggedy Andy. It might be Sarah."

She pulled up a chair and sat behind my shoulder. "How can you find out?"

"I think if I win the bid I can get the address of the seller. How else would buyers know where to send the money?"

"What if it's a post office box? That won't help much."

"I'll deal with that if I get that far," I said.

"You're sure you aren't going to end up spending a fortune on a doll you don't want?"

"I'm not sure. Got to try, that's all."

As it turned out, I couldn't bid unless I was a registered e-Bay person. For that, I needed to provide an e-mail address, a public name, like Mamadoll, and a secret name, plus select a unique password. Then e-Bay would let me do deals. I'd have to have my account confirmed by them first. "I'll have to use your e-mail address," I told Deborah.

"Let's switch chairs," she said and assumed command.

She filled out blanks in the form on her screen, clicked the mouse, and sent it. There was no telling how soon we'd get a confirmation. If e-Bay was an automated system, it should come quickly. If they depended on humans to do that bookkeeping, who would work at-- I checked my watch-- three in the morning?

Luckily, it was an automated system. The computer startled me by talking: "You have mail!"

Deborah swiveled the chair to face me. "We're in. Now, what do you want to bid?"

I swallowed hard. "Five hundred and fifty-one dollars," I said. "Try that."

The bidding wouldn't close until noon, long after we had left for Arthur's funeral, so we wouldn't know until we got back from the funerals if we'd won the bid. In the meantime, I had enough of a story to tell the relatives that would sound authentic. "I've found Sarah," I could say, almost with conviction. "She's alive." I hoped I wasn't mistaken. In any case, if Sarah were alive, there'd be no point in anyone killing anybody else, at least for now.

Unless they went after Sarah-- if they could find her. For now all I had as an e-Bay code name. No guarantee that Mamadoll was Sarah.

Deborah logged off of AOL and shut down her computer. "Are you ready to go to bed now?"

"Yeh. You were showing me something a little while ago. Let's have another look at that."

37.

I don't think I got more than three hours sleep before the alarm went off and we were on our way with time only for cold cereal while the coffee maker did its thing. I filled a thermos and packed two insulated sipper cups for the trip. I made sure to tuck the manila envelope with the possible keys to the Rottman cottage in the side pocket of my overnight bag.

Deborah reminded me to pack my prescriptions. I had graduated in my last year on the job from Tums to real stomach medicine. Not that life among my relatives was any less stressful. When I was still working outside the home nobody tried to run me over or put a bomb in my car. This can make for genuine dyspepsia.

Before we left I called the Lansing police and left a message for Officer Finelli to inform him that we were going to a funeral and would probably be away overnight. I didn't say where. He hadn't cautioned me not to leave town. I hoped the Lansing police would keep an eye on the house for us. Since he suspected me of drug dealing, maybe his budget had room for some watchers.

Watchers or not, I wasn't taking any chances. Deborah had made sure that the garage door was closed when she parked her car, but I insisted she pop the hood of her Camry so I could inspect the engine for bombs before she hit the starter. I didn't want a repeat performance.

I admit I held my breath and closed my eyes when she turned the ignition key. I did not experience instant death. The garage door opened and we were off, a repeat trip to Hobart, only now we knew the way. Should be easier.

At least this time we knew where the exit ramp was off the I-94 and weren't caught between two menacing eighteen wheelers. Even so, we were delayed by construction. When we got to Cecile and Arthur's house, she had already left. Nuts.

Not to worry. Nosy neighbor Ollie had seen us pull up. I had hardly turned away from Cecile's door, frustrated, when Ollie came out of her house, all dressed up in what I suspected was her best funeral outfit.

"Cecile told me to watch for you," Ollie said. "She had to leave early to make some arrangements. I'll show you the way to the funeral home." Without an invitation she got in the back seat of the Camry.

"We won't be coming back," I explained over my shoulder. "We've got a double header today."

"I know," Ollie said. "I'll find a ride."

I was sure she would.

It turned out to be the Pearce Funeral Home, a modern building with plenty of parking. The mortician who met us was a young guy who didn't look Jewish and was plainly uneasy. I guess it takes practice to put on that special, solemn demeanor suitable for all denominations. He had a little box of black yarmulkes ready for the Jewish mourners if I was of that faith but he was plainly uncertain about how he should offer them. "Thank you," I said, putting one on. I had forgotten to stick mine in my pocket before we left Lansing. "I hope you got my size."

"They come in sizes?" he asked, confused. That confirmed my guess. This kid definitely wasn't Jewish.

I didn't bother to tell him it was a joke.

Cecile was there in her big hair, but wearing a modest black outfit with a flower. Even though she had plenty of time to prepare mentally for Arthur's death, her eyes were red and she kept touching the end of her nose with a tissue. Deborah moved right up to Cecile to give her moral support. I gave her a solemn hug.

I was surprised at the number of people who showed up for Arthur's memorial service. I tried to guess who they might be and which might be detectives hoping to catch an arsonist who came to gloat. A couple of men in sport jackets looked like they might be Arthur's partners or competitors. Some of the young women in the audience had that pale, used look of hookers and B girls who never see the sun. Makeup intended for stripping on the bar doesn't look right in normal lighting. Most of the mourners were men, working stiffs who looked like they might be regulars at the Gents Club. I guessed Arthur had mixed with the patrons. He hadn't just stayed in his office to count money.

It was a big crowd. I hadn't known Arthur and didn't have a high opinion of him, but plenty of people who cared about him did.

It didn't take me long to pick out the cops in plain clothes. They hung back so they could watch the room. I walked up to them and introduced myself as if I thought they were friends of the family. "I'm Adam Rottman, cousin of the deceased. Were you some of Arthur's regular customers?"

Both men reluctantly shook hands, but didn't give their names. They weren't wearing yarmulkes. I guessed Hobart didn't have any Jewish policemen. The ear pieces they wore told me it wasn't Walkmans playing hard rock music in their pockets. I didn't see any bulges that might look like 9 mm Glocks, the favorite police hand gun.

"Keep a good eye," I said to let them know I wouldn't blow their cover. "You might want to have a guard on the parking lot. Someone put a bomb in my Volvo this week. The Lansing police removed it."

Their reaction was noncommittal. Maybe they'd been told, maybe not.

"You coming to the other funeral, too? Miriam's, in Chicago?"

The answer was a quiet negative.

I was right. At least in this case the Indiana detectives stayed on their side of the line. I wondered who would be watching the mourners at Miriam's memorial service.

The police presence made me feel safer.

The rabbi turned out to be a woman in her thirties. She had close-cropped hair and a butch look. I guessed if she were a lesbian, she would have more sympathy for this crowd of people society looks down upon. It was a brief memorial and almost entirely in English, a Reform service.

One of Arthur's friends did get up to share his experience of Arthur. Seems they were fishing partners who, after the Gent's club closed early in the morning, would have the three dollar breakfast special at Jamal's Amman Middle Eastern cafe, then jump in a jeep and look for bluegills.

The personal revelations reminded me of Sadie's Shiva reception. I didn't get to know much about Arthur, either, until he was dead. Arthur sounded like a nice guy. I had an old fishing rod in the garage. Maybe we could have gone on a bluegill hunt. This would never happen now. I might have enjoyed knowing Arthur, in spite of his volatile personality. I guessed he had been bipolar, too.

True to his word, Harold did not make the trip from Indianapolis. I didn't expect Schmuel, so his absence was no surprise. Deborah and I got to meet Cecile's mother and her brother. I guessed the rest of the Golds would be at Miriam's memorial service, miles away.

Everyone, Jew and Gentile both, recognized the twenty-third psalm. For the strangers, the rest of the service was unfamiliar. Before the kaddish memorial prayer the rabbi paused tactfully for the benefit of the non-Jews to explain that the kaddish doesn't mention death or resurrection but sanctifies and glorifies the Name of God. She read the English translation as well as the Hebrew.

I didn't spot Jake until after the kaddish memorial prayer. Jake was at the back of the chapel wearing the same pin stripe he'd had on at Sadie's Shiva reception. He looked worried.

"Glad you could make it," Jake said. "Arthur had a bad temper but he was OK. It's too bad." Something else was worrying him.

"I didn't tell you over the phone that there have been two attempts on my life."

I expected Jake to make some tough guy remark. He didn't. "Tell me about it."

"Someone tried to run me down, like Millie, and someone put a bomb in my car. Only reason I lived to tell about it is the Volvo had a dead battery."

"This is not good," Jake said.

"There's something you're not telling me," I said.

Jake looked around. He had spotted the detectives, too. I guess he's had plenty of practice. "This isn't the place to talk about it. You going to Miriam's service?"

"Yes, and then on to Waldheim's."

Jake hadn't expected that. "You driving all the way back to Michigan after that? You should stay in Chicago a few days."

I shook my head. "Deborah's clients would be sleepless without her. She has to tell them bedtime stories."

"Why doesn't she just give them prescriptions for knock-out drops?"

"She doesn't write prescriptions," I reminded him again. "Deborah isn't a doctor."

Jake apologized. "Look, we'll talk later. Come to my place after the graveside service. You can stay over. Since the kids left we got plenty of room."

All this was normal conversation, like there wasn't someone trying to kill us all, or at least me. Maybe pretending that everything is A-OK is what Deborah would call a defense mechanism as in "Have a cup of tea? Oh, and don't sit in front of the window." If Arthur could be torched, Miriam shot in the back, and me car bombed, who knows? While we sat telling family stories someone might spray Jake's house with a machine gun.

What if Jake was behind all this? Did we dare stay the night with someone who might be engineering these deaths? It would be like moving into the spider's den. We're not Moslems. If we were Moslems we'd be guaranteed three nights of safety even in the tent of our worst enemy. After that it would be open season.

We didn't have that custom. Staying over at Jake's was something I definitely did not want to do. "Would your wife approve? I wouldn't invite anyone over unless Deborah knew about it." I didn't know his wife.

"She's home now setting up for a reception for the family. We offered. Miriam's place is, well..."

Jake didn't finish his sentence. He was being tactful. I had heard that the Jakobis were not well off but I had never seen their home. Like they said in The Godfather movie, it was an offer I couldn't refuse.

38.

Before we left the Hobart funeral parlor I insisted that Deborah open the hood of the Camry. "You really are nervous, aren't you?" Deborah asked.

"Humor me," I said and pretended to be checking the oil. No bombs. "If we're being watched, always checking under the hood may discourage them."

Deborah tried to joke about it, but it was a thin facade. "It's time I got you on my couch." She was worried, too.

It wasn't possible for the funeral entourage to stick together for the long drive to Waldheim's. Someone had prepared a little map with directions, but only the closest of Arthur's friends would hazard the freeways all the way to Chicago's west side, even using the I-90 bypass.

When we got to the Waldheim chapel I was surprised to see the lot full of taxi cabs. Some of the drivers were demonstrating with signs demanding more police protection for cab drivers. A television truck was parked nearby with its dish antennas in the open for business position. This was a media event.

Because of the cab drivers' demonstration there were a couple of police cars parked nearby and men in blue ready to intervene if things got too vociferous. I didn't spot any plains clothes cops.

We had to run the gauntlet of demonstrators to get inside. The Waldheim memorial chapel was another world from the Hobart funeral parlor. Waldheim's place was kosher. No doubt about who should put on a yarmulke here.

Miriam's mourners were different, too. Though she hadn't worked for the cab company for very long, the cabbies sent a delegation of massive support. Being shot and robbed was an occupational hazard they could all relate to. The funeral chapel was so packed that the proprietors had to slide open a folding partition at the back to extend the room.

The rabbi hired for Arthur's service was reform and a woman. The rabbi at Waldheim's was male, elderly and Orthodox. I hadn't realized that Miriam's husband was not only a meat cutter, but a kosher butcher. It was a different world from the sleazy Calumet city crowd with its bartenders, B-girls and hookers.

Jake, knowing the city, had beat us to the place. He separated me from the crowd. Deborah clung to me like glue to make sure she heard everything and put it in her professional mental computer.

"About this attempt on your life," Jake began. "I may be responsible, sort of indirectly, you might say."

"What do you mean? How can you be indirectly responsible for a bomb?"

"It's a long shot, maybe twenty to one odds," Jake explained, revealing his bookmaker experience. "I remember when I was in LA for Sadie's funeral I was asked how someone could contract for a hit."

"Who asked you?"

Jake wriggled like one of Arthur's bluegills trying to get off the hook. "People think that because they call me Mafia Man I'm an authority on that sort of activity. It wasn't a right out straight forward inquiry, you understand. It was oblique, slipped into the conversation sort of off hand, not serious, but now that you tell me attempts were made on your life, it rings a bell."

Deborah was studying Jake carefully, hanging on every word. "So who was ringing your bell?"

"Sylvia. Schmuel's wife."

"But she's out in California. What do they do nowadays, mail order contracts for murder?" I remembered my kidding Harold about Murder Incorporated dot com. I wasn't convinced. For all I knew Jake's story was a smoke screen to divert my suspicion away from himself.

Jake tried not to talk down to my ignorant self, but he was having difficulty. "If you was hiding in South America under a fake name you could be found. No professional criminal is gonna to stick his neck out and do these things himself. The pros don't get caught."

"What about John Gotti?" I asked, remembering the famous trial.

"Too high a profile," Jake explained. "His ego got too big for him so he became an irritant. You don't want to become an irritant. Then the feds go after you like bloodhounds. The last thing you want is a prosecutor who has a hard on for you."

I remembered Officer Finelli's suspicions of me. "I'll keep that in mind next time I do something criminal."

Deborah brought Jake back to the point. "So you say Sylvia wanted to know how someone did a contract for murder?"

"Yeh, in a manner of speaking."

"What did you tell her?"

Jake bowed his head and shrugged. "I gave her a phone number. That's all. I don't know if she called or if she did anything about it. Maybe she forgot."

"Maybe it was you," I said. Jake was still my prime suspect.

"Me? God forbid. I'm not interested in Sadie's million."

That I couldn't believe. Anybody would be interested in inheriting a million smackeroos. Maybe not Bill Gates. That's another ball game.

Deborah looked at me. "It must cost plenty to contract for murder. Adam, I thought you said Sylvia and Schmuel are broke."

What could I say? I didn't know Schmuel's financial status. "Maybe they got a cash advance."

The commotion outside in the parking lot made the atmosphere inside tense. Miriam's family had formed a short receiving line. I learned her husband the meat cutter and kosher butcher was Michayel, pronounced in the Hebrew fashion, not Mike.

"I'm Adam Rottman, Miriam's cousin."

He took my hand. Michayel was short and stocky, like maybe he was Russian. I noticed he had lost the ends of two of his fingers. Those bone saws can do a lot of damage. "I heard about you."

I wondered what Miriam had told him. Nothing bad, I hoped, but considering that anything Harold did rubbed off on me, I wasn't optimistic. "I'm sorry my brother Harold couldn't make it," I said.

"What about your sister?" Michayel asked.

"She's still missing, presumed dead, but I have a lead. I think she'll turn up."

Michayel in his grief did not seem interested.

Their son, Ira, their daughter Rebecca and her husband all shook hands as we made our condolences. I whispered to Deborah, "I hope that Miriam's killing is a coincidence that has nothing to do with Aunt Sadie's tontine. It would be terrible if Michayel and his family blamed me for her death."

She gave me a disapproving look. "I don't think Michayel is the devious type, Adam. This isn't about you."

"When one person in the human family is harmed, we are all diminished," I said.

The service was starting so we took our seats at the front, close to Miriam's immediate family.

This time the service was heavy on the Hebrew. There was no explanation for the uninitiated. If you didn't know what it was all about, maybe you didn't belong.

It was only when it was over and we patiently shuffled through the crowd toward the exit that I spotted someone I hadn't expected to see.

I nudged Deborah. "Look who's here."

Schmuel had come after all. Had he brought Sylvia? After what I had gone through in the last week I was immediately suspicious. If Schmuel had ordered the aborted car bombing, was he here to oversee the job himself and move a couple of steps closer to Sadie's money? With me and Jake within easy reach, that left only Harold in Indianapolis. Knocking off my brother Harold would be easy: just poison one of those foot long sandwiches he sends out for so he can eat lunch at his desk. Glutton that he is it might look like he choked.

I remembered that you can't kill someone and still get your inheritance. That would be a deterrent, I told myself. But dumb criminals still do murders in spite of the death penalty. Most murders were irrational acts, done in a fit of rage or other madness. I told myself if Schmuel tried to shoot someone he wouldn't know which end of the gun the bullets come out of. I wasn't convinced.

"What?" Deborah asked.

"I must be talking to myself. I'm sorry, Deborah. I'm so distracted. I'm glad you're driving. I'd probably run a red light."

On the way out we were handed a brochure about the Waldheim organization and one of those magnetic funeral flags to put on the car for the funeral procession to the cemetery.

I'd been identified. Someone took me firmly by the shoulder. "What?" I was startled. A Waldheim official pinned a bit of black cloth to the lapel of my jacket and cut it. I had forgotten the ritual. A mourner is supposed to wear sackcloth and ashes, or at least rent his garments. The bit of cut ribbon saved the wardrobe.

The Waldheim organization, I learned, was not one cemetery but three hundred. The one we were going to was the old one. The plots where they were planting Arthur and Miriam were bought ages ago by great grandpa Isaac Gold, the horse thief who made good. According to the map it was off Des Plaines avenue not far from the interchange of the I-90 and the 294. All we had to do was follow the hearse.

39.

Driving in to the grave site was like entering another world. If we hadn't been behind the hearse we would never have found it. This was not prime real estate, not then and not now. It was between an old railway and a branch of the Chicago river, more like a drainage ditch and about as attractive. A dusty dirt road, little more than a trail, led from the rusted iron gate. The Gold family plot was way at the back.

The old Waldheim cemetery is a crowded place with narrow paths. Except for those whose few surviving descendants bother to visit, the graves are unkempt, overgrown. Some of the grave stones have pictures of the decreased, pictures often smashed by vandals. Jewish cemeteries seem to be fair game for cowardly anti-Semitic thugs who pick on the dead because they can't defend themselves.

I had only been to the Gold family plot once when grandpa Abe Gold was buried. Now the last available graves were open, so close together that they needed only one hole. When Miriam and Arthur were laid to rest there would be no more vacancies. Where would the rest of us be put?

I realized it was time I made my own arrangements. We all know we are going to die eventually, but how many of us suspect someone wants to speed up the process? What with two attempts on my life, I might be needing a grave site soon.

Both rabbis were there, Arthur's female Reform and Miriam's Orthodox male, but in spite of their professional connection watching them confer about who would go first was like watching Yassar Arafat negotiating with Arya Sharon.

The Waldheim grave diggers were uncertain. Hispanic, they conferred in barely audible Spanish about their job. Their equipment for lowering a coffin was made to span one open grave, not to do a double header. They had substituted a couple of raw planks.

Down in the bottom of the open graves I saw the prescribed concrete vaults were shoulder to shoulder. Brother and sister would be close enough to hold hands. On the outside of each grave was a mound of earth, discreetly covered by a piece of Astroturf to hide the reminder that in a few minutes it would be our duty to shovel dirt into the graves.

Cecile asked me if I would be a pall bearer for Arthur. That explained why I'd had the ribbon pinned on my lapel. I couldn't help remembering the last time I had seen Arthur and Miriam was when they were getting off the plane at O'Hare. Now they were both dead, only a day apart. Aunt Sadie, I thought aloud, what have you done? You and your accursed tontine.

Schmuel had also been given the honor of schlepping Arthur's coffin from the hearse. We stood facing each other across the coffin. I couldn't resist a comment. "That's two down, Schmuel. Who's next?"

Schmuel gave me a frightened look. For once he wasn't wearing his sunglasses and I could see the look in his eyes.

"You got your plot picked out in Tinseltown?" I asked. "Out at Mount Sinai near Aunt Sadie, maybe?"

Schmuel's voice was hoarse. "I hadn't thought about it."

His look suggested that he thought I was behind all this and he might be next. This was not the cocky SOB who was eager to get his hands on Sarah's Raggedies.

"Now let's lift together, gentlemen," the English-speaking attendant from Waldheim advised. With practice, I guess you could learn to carry a coffin without throwing your back out or getting a hernia. I hoped not to have that much practice.

The Waldheim attendant passed out little booklets with the prayers. Whatever cool conference the two rabbis had had, they managed to do a nice, joint graveside service.

I already knew the kaddish by heart but when we got to it I couldn't help crying. I told myself I wasn't crying for them, because I hardly knew Arthur or Miriam; I was crying for myself. Deborah gripped my hand but I pulled away to get out the tissue she had discreetly slipped into my pocket.

Nobody got hysterical and leaped into the grave as my grandmother did when grandpa Abe was buried. Cecile was a picture of quiet grief. Michayel stood hunched up with his kids beside him. He didn't need to consult the prayer booklet. With his

145

daughter married and son at college, his future would be an empty household to come home to at the end of the working day.

The last ritual is that dreaded moment, the little shovel of dirt.

I didn't have to do that part, and hung back, numb. Schmuel bent to pick up a handful of dirt for the graves.

And who was the last? Sure enough, she had come. It was Sylvia, dressed in an expensive black outfit, with a veil. No wonder I hadn't spotted her before. Sylvia planted a high heeled foot on the spade, dug deep, and threw in several shovels of dirt. It was if to say, "There. You're not coming up."

I hung back to watch the Hispanic laborers use a machine to hoist the concrete vault lids and lower them into place. I didn't stick around to watch the graves filled with dirt.

Who knows about the spirits of the dead? If I knew the Golds, even a closed coffin with six feet of earth on top of a concrete, sealed vault wouldn't hold them back. It was that Gold chromosome. Considering how many Golds were buried in this family plot at Waldheim, they could have a chorus of vengeful voices.

Deborah had said we were all bipolar. I wondered if ghosts were bipolar, too.

40.

The number of mourners had dwindled when we left the funeral chapel and fewer still accepted Jake's invitation to run up to his home in Deerfield. Deerfield is beyond Skokie, and every mile we drove north on the freeway made our return trip to Lansing that much farther. We were definitely not going to make it back that night and would have to stop somewhere en route. I didn't want to stay at Jake's. No way.

Jake's house in Deerfield was not as sumptuous as I had imagined. I guess I expected something Tudor with a high fence, an electric gate, and Dobermans. Instead it was an older fifties style mid-scale split level with a sunken garage and bedrooms over that.

We were a select group that assembled at Jake's. Deborah's Camry took up the last few feet of the driveway. I wondered how Schmuel and Sylvia had gotten from the airport to Waldheim's and saw they had rented a car, a two door white Neon they parked at the curb.

I had never met Jake's wife, Cindy. She greeted us at the door with a 500 watt smile that must have made her dentist rich. Cindy is taller than Jake, nearly six feet, and has a bosom that needs no implants. If they go dancing, even if he wears those elevated shoes Jake's nose must fit right into Cindy's cleavage, nice work if you can get it. I guessed that Cindy outweighs Jake, too, by a few pounds, but being tall carries it well.

The only thing notable about the furnishings of Jake and Cindy's house was her collection of Hummel figurines. They were all over the place. On a wall where some other family might have books, Cindy had a glass display case, rows on rows of those little porcelain boys and girls.

"So you're a collector," I said, pointing to the Hummels. "My sister Sarah is a collector, too."

"Does she collect these?"

"No. Her schtick is Raggedy Ann and Andy dolls. She must have hundreds."

Cindy plainly couldn't see the attraction of stuffed cloth dolls. "Collecting is a disease," I said and immediately felt bad for being tactless. I introduced Deborah.

That over with, Deborah whispered, "You have a very diverse family, Adam."

"I'm afraid we don't fit the usual Jewish stereotypes. No doctors here, no dentists, no Sigmund Freuds or violin protégés. The only lawyer is my brother. We're just plain folks, like anybody else. Except for the occasional gangster."

In fact, we were virtually strangers. None of the cousins were friends. We were bound by accidents of birth that made us all descendants of great grandpa Isaac Gold.

What we had that bound us like chained slaves jettisoned at sea was a common curse. Which of us would be next?

Schmuel tried to recover his usual nastiness. "I heard you had a car bomb."

"Yes, who told you that?"

Schmuel shrugged. "Everybody knows about it. How come you didn't blow up?"

"The battery was dead. I hope you're not disappointed."

If he was, he didn't show it. "Who do you think put it there?"

"Harold thinks it was a professional, murder by mail order. What do you think?"

Schmuel shrugged. Cindy had set out a box of Godiva chocolates on the coffee table. Schmuel took one, bit the corner, didn't like it and put it back in the box. "What do I know from car bombs? Goornisht." Nothing at all. "If your brother knows all about that stuff, maybe he arranged it. I wouldn't put it past him."

I didn't think the remark worthy of an answer. Harold might have helped Sadie with her pernicious plans, but I didn't see him capable of murdering his own brother.

Cindy had laid out quite a spread with genuine lox, something you don't find in Lansing, heaps of corned beef and pastrami for sandwiches to make with real Chicago rye bread or bagels, a bowl of huge kosher dill pickles. I wasn't sure whether we were supposed to slice them for our sandwiches or chomp them like a special treat. I took a bite of one and put it on my plate. The garlic was so strong it made my eyes water. This was the real thing.

On a sideboard was an array of liquor bottles and kosher creme soda and berry pop for the designated drivers. We hid our lack of conversation by wrapping our mouths around sandwiches.

Michayel was closed in on himself. "I went to the cab company office," he said to no one in particular. "To pick up Miriam's things and get her pay. Can you believe it? The company docked her the twenty-four dollars that was stolen."

We all agreed it was an insensitive act. I hoped the company owners weren't Jewish.

Cindy Gold took Deborah by the arm. "You'll stay, of course. Jake's told me about what's been going on, but I'd like to hear your side of the story, Sadie's funeral, and all this tontine business."

Deborah begged off. "I have clients to see tomorrow."

"Can't you cancel?"

While they were dickering about it, Jake took me aside. "I got to talk to you, Adam."

He pulled me into the study. There, again instead of books, the shelves were full of porcelain figurines. There were small shipping boxes on the floor beside the desk and a roll of bubble wrap. I was reminded of the mess at Sarah's apartment in LA, except Cindy was not out of control.

The computer on the desk was on, a screen saver of animated Hummel figurines that played tag across the screen. I had seen a screen saver with a cat chasing a mouse. Maybe some programmer had substituted animated boy and girl Hummel figures. I wondered who was trying to catch who. "Your computer?" I asked Jake.

"No. This is Cindy's. I use a laptop for the business." Jake closed the study door behind us and reached inside the jacket of his pin stripe suit.

I drew back, startled and afraid.

"I want you to have this," Jake said, and pressed it into my hand. "Careful, it's loaded."

I held it up gingerly, afraid to leave my fingerprints on it. "What is it?"

"It's a gun, stupid."

"I know it's a gun." All I know about guns I saw in the movies. John Wayne wouldn't have strapped this to his cowboy outfit. "Not a revolver." I studied it, lots of chrome, not as heavy as I expected. The ones Finelli and the other Lansing police carried on their belts looked like they'd dislocate your spine if you didn't balance them with a knight stick, radio, and handcuffs on the other hip.

"It's only a .32," Jake explained. "Small caliber. A woman's gun. Women used to carry them in their muffs."

I remembered muffs, big fur hand warmers with inside pockets for change, and, I had just learned, an occasional gat. "I don't have a muff."

My lame joke exasperated Jake. "For God's sake, Adam, if people are trying to kill you, you should carry some heat."

"I don't know anything about guns."

Jake gave me a look like I must have Downs syndrome or something. "Don't be such a wimp. Just don't point it at anybody unless you intend to shoot. See, here's the safety. This is on, this is off. The magazine holds six shots. I can give you a box of ammunition."

He showed me how to eject the magazine, that before it would shoot you first had to chamber a round by pulling back the top. After that it reloaded itself. I protested. "I don't want it. I don't have a permit."

"You can get one, Adam. Somebody made an attempt on your life. That's grounds for a concealed weapon permit."

I found myself shaking at the thought. "All right. Thanks, Jake. I appreciate your concern. Sorry if I seem stupid. Let me pay you for it." I hoped it wasn't expensive. I didn't have much cash. "You take VISA?"

"Forget it. It's a gift."

Kidding aside, I wondered, in my continued suspicion, if this weren't a stolen pistol, or one used in a killing on the streets of Chicago, a weapon with a history of death that now had my fingerprints on it. Maybe Jake was setting me up. Maybe the gun wasn't loaded after all, and I was meant to aim it at someone and oblige them to shoot first. Then whoever bumped me off could claim self defense. I put it in my jacket pocket. Its weight, small though it was, was conspicuous.

"Not in that pocket," Jake said, impatient. Like he was dressing a small boy, he unbuttoned my jacket, put his arms around me, and tucked the pistol in my waistband at the small of my back. "There. Now no one will notice unless you dance with a female detective."

"I'll try to avoid that." I have to admit, being armed made me feel different. Now I understood why Jake had that funny swagger.

In his business he probably always packed some heat, as they say in the old B movies. I floated back into the dining room on cat feet, reborn like some secret agent with license to kill. It was a feeling that didn't last.

Deborah saw through my new role immediately. "What is it, Adam?"

I winked at her and whispered out of the corner of my mouth. "Jake gave me a gun. He says we need protection." I took her hand and pressed it to the small of my back so she could feel it herself.

She was startled.

As it turned out, this was not the only startling development.

41.

After making a respectful appearance, eaten a sandwich, nibbled one or two Godiva chocolates from the box, a couple of the guests got up to leave. As if on signal, all the rest, except for the cousins and spouses, decided to leave, too. Cecile got up first, pleading a long drive back to Hobart.

"Wait," I said. "We haven't talked. Have the police found out who set the fire?"

The spark had gone out of Cecile's eyes since the arson. "There's an investigation. The police interviewed the bartenders and the bouncer. They're talking to the waitresses. If they don't get any leads from them they say they'll go through the list of everyone who paid their tab with a credit card. I'm afraid if they don't get results quickly nothing will come of it. Catching whoever it was isn't going to bring Arthur back."

I turned to Michayel. "Do the police have any clues about Miriam's case?" I almost said "killer."

Michayel had a mouthful of pastrami sandwich. His son Ira intervened. "I think they're doing ballistic tests to see if she was shot with the same gun that killed two other cab drivers. They also have the dispatcher's tape. Since the other murders all the calls are recorded."

It sounded to me like the deaths were not related, that two Gold cousins being killed in the same week was just a coincidence. If the ballistic tests didn't match and if the passenger Miriam had picked up had flagged her down or had walked up to her cab stand, there'd be no recorded voice of the passenger.

I hoped the deaths were a coincidence, but still suspected someone had ordered them. Harold wouldn't do that. In control of Sadie's trust, Harold already had control of Sadie's money. It could be someone in this room, I thought, and studied all their faces.

Cecile excused herself. It was a long drive back to Hobart. She was followed by Michayel and his kids. None of them were on Sadie's tontine list. Once they were gone, I thought it advisable to have a serious talk with Jake and Schmuel. I wanted to put an end to the trouble. In fact, I only made things worse.

The six of us were sitting in the living room, looking washed out from two funerals and all that driving in the Chicago traffic. I stood up and got their attention. "I had a talk with Harold about this crazy tontine thing," I began. "You should know that Sadie's estate is administered in Indiana, a common law state."

"So?" Sylvia asked. "What about it?"

"That means if Sarah's body doesn't turn up, Sadie's tontine doesn't take effect for seven years. None of us can get the money for at least that long. Then, of course, only the last survivor collects. That might be thirty years from now, or more. Golds have good genes."

"It might be even less time, considering that two Golds were buried today," Jake said.

"But if Sarah isn't dead," I ventured to say. "The tontine won't kick in for years and years. I suggest we just forget about it."

Sylvia's eyes popped. "Forget one million dollars?"

"Might not be that much in twenty years, considering inheritance taxes and how inflation reduces purchasing power. It might have shrunk to only two hundred and fifty thousand. That's not enough to get excited about."

Schmuel studied his glass of soda. He was drinking the berry pop. "Quarter of a million is still a lot of money, and there's the interest."

I corrected him. "Remember, the principal doesn't grow. The interest goes to Sarah."

"If she's alive," Sylvia said.

She sounded to me like she knew better. Maybe she had something to do with Sarah's driving her Volkswagen into the Los Angeles river.

"Even if she isn't alive, the interest goes into her bank account until the courts declare her dead. I think she is alive," I said. "We just haven't found her." I turned to Jake's wife. "Cindy, could you help me with something?"

Cindy got up and I asked her to follow me into the study. I closed the door behind me. "All these figurines of yours. Do you buy and sell on e-Bay?"

"Sure."

"Do you know how to get a seller's address?"

She knew.

"Go to the Raggedy Ann doll list. See if someone named Mamadoll is selling something."

It didn't take her long to call up that page on e-Bay. There they were again, only this time a somewhat different mix of Raggedies. It looked like little ones were going today. Sure enough, one was being offered by a seller called Mamadoll. "That could be her," I said, pointing to the entry on the computer screen. "Can you find out her particulars, like her address?"

"That's not hard," Cindy said.

"Not hard for you. You do this all the time. I haven't the first clue," I said. Standing hunched over the back of her chair like that was uncomfortable. I pulled up a chair and sat down, but when I did that silly gun stuck me in the back. I took it out of my waist band and laid it on the desk next to the computer.

"What's that for?" Cindy asked.

"Jake gave it to me. Protection."

Cindy wasn't surprised. Guns seemed to be a normal part of her life. She had to click on a couple of e-Bay links and wait while another page loaded off the internet, but finally there it was: Mamadoll. A post office box in New Buffalo, Michigan. But the name on e-Bay's list wasn't Sarah Gold.

"It's not her," Cindy said.

"Is there some way a person can sell without giving their own name?"

"Sure. You can have a proxy, someone who takes stuff on consignment and sells it for you."

I leaned forward so I could bring my face closer to Cindy's. I could smell her perfume. Jake was a lucky guy. "If you had to move your collection out of here, what would you do?"

"I'd stay with the collection," Cindy said. "Otherwise I couldn't buy and sell."

"My feeling exactly. Sarah's doll collection was moved to the old family place in Michiana Shores. The mailing address on the Michigan side of the state line is New Buffalo. That's a few miles away. If Sarah's hiding out at the cottage, afraid to show herself, she might have a friend take care of the mail for her in New Buffalo. Can I use your phone?"

I'd tried calling the cottage before but there was never any answer. Nobody there. Or nobody daring to pick up. I didn't have my address book with me, so had to call the information operator.

A bored operator asked, "What city, please?"

"New Buffalo, Michigan. Harold Rottman." I spelled it.

Fortunately the number was listed. An automated voice recited it twice in robot tones, then offered to connect for a fee. I opted for that and held my breath. I heard the beeping of the automatic dialer, then got a busy signal.

"She's there!" I said, triumphant. "I bet she's on line with her computer, selling stuff."

I thought I heard the door shut behind me. I was sure I had closed it. Had someone been eavesdropping?

"It could be your brother," Cindy suggested.

"It could be Harold, but the only place he goes is to his office. He even has lunch delivered. It's got to be Sarah. Cindy, please don't say anything about this to anybody." I hurried back to the living room. Everyone was still seated as before except Sylvia. "Where's Sylvia?"

"Bathroom." Jake said. "Whatcha find out?"

I suddenly realized that whoever tried to kill me could find out Sarah's whereabouts just as I had. If she were found dead at the cottage there'd be no waiting seven years for a death certificate. The post office box address wouldn't delay anyone who knew enough to look in the New Buffalo phone book for a Rottman. Did the phone book give the street number? Did it just say Michiana Shores, or did it mention Lake Shore Drive, Stop forty? If it were that specific, it was just a matter of cruising down that block to check names on the mail boxes.

"We've got to go," I told Deborah. "Right away."

"What?"

Jake protested. "Hey, I thought you were staying over."

"Sorry." I made apologies.

Cindy hustled about. "We've so much food. Take something with you. Jake and I will never eat all of this. Lox doesn't freeze well. I'll make you a couple sandwiches."

Pausing at the doorway with a bag of sandwiches and two enormous kosher dill pickles, I remembered the gun. "I forgot something," I said. "Be right back."

I returned to the study. The room was dark, except for the Hummels playing tag on the computer screen. I didn't need to turn on the light to see that the pistol was gone.

42.

The air was warm and humid when we left Jake's house, a smell of rain and a few sprinkles. Not good. With all those oil drips on the expressway in the first hours of rain driving would be hazardous.

This time I was in such a hurry to get out of there that I didn't ask Deborah to open the hood of the Camry. We were lucky. The bomb people hadn't followed us from the cemetery. The car started and we didn't blow up.

"What's the rush?" Deborah asked as she pulled the Camry out of the driveway.

"Sarah's at the lake. I'm sure of it. Whoever was contracted to kill me might be on the way to the cottage to get Sarah."

"Seems far fetched to me, Adam."

"Just humor me. Aren't you curious? After all the trouble I went to in LA to find her? She's my sister for God's sake."

"It'll be midnight by the time we get there," Deborah said. "Which way is the freeway?"

I remembered the route. "Keep going straight." I wondered what the traffic was like at this hour. When we were kids it took over two hours to drive from Michigan City to Chicago. That was before the interstates, the Indiana Toll Road and the Skyway were built. They shortened the trip to only forty minutes. But Deerfield was another forty minutes to the north. With Chicago's traffic congestion it could take longer than before.

"We can't just keep trying to call her to warn her if she's on the internet tying up the phone line," I said. "That would waste time."

"Why don't you try again? I have to get gas," Deborah said. "You can call Sarah from a gas station."

She pulled up at a brightly lit Texaco station to fill up. This was big city stuff. Cash only. You had to pay in advance by sliding your money into a little box under the bullet proof window. The sign on the window said "Smile. You are under 24 hour surveillance." After you paid, the attendant set the pump so it would cut off when your deposit ran out. Nobody was going to tank up and run for it from this station.

I said, "regular unleaded," shoved a twenty dollar bill into the slot, looked up at the camera and gave it the one finger salute. "Hi, Mom!" To the attendant: "You got a phone here?"

The attendant was a kid barely out of high school. I guessed his parents were glad he worked inside a fortification. Late night gas stations were dangerous places to work. "Over there." He pointed.

The phone was outdoors on a post. To discourage drug dealers with beepers, a sign said "This phone does not take incoming calls." By now drug dealers with any style had their own cell phones. Unfortunately, this pay phone didn't do outgoing calls, either. Someone had unscrewed the mouthpiece.

Fortunately, traffic wasn't as bad as I'd feared. The drizzle turned into a light rain. Deborah expertly avoided the slow moving cars and stayed back behind the semi trucks that threw up a spray of greasy water. The film on the windshield had to be washed every few minutes. I hoped there was enough washer fluid in the tank.

When we got near Michigan City I directed Deborah to the old highway. No sightseeing on the lake road this time. That was too slow. I almost missed the grade crossing over the railway track where so many people had been killed before the installation of a crossing gate. "Take the next left," I told Deborah. "There... that's the one."

At that time of the year Michiana Shores is deserted. Later all the summer residents would show up with kids and beach toys. Most of the houses were dark. I was grateful that a street light had been put up at Stop forty. The old bus stop had a roof, a couple of benches where people could wipe the sand off their feet when they climbed the stairs from the beach, and a water fountain.

We pulled up in front of the garage and parked. Looking up from the lake road I couldn't see much. The blinds were all drawn.

Deborah got out of the car and stretched. Her neck was sore from the concentration on night driving on unfamiliar roads. "It doesn't look like there's anyone here. You sure you didn't dial a wrong number?"

I took the flashlight from the glove compartment and got the manila envelope with the three most likely keys. "Let's try the garage door first," I said.

Klutz that I am, I dropped two of the keys into the sand outside the garage door and had to find them again and wipe them off.

The third key fit. I turned the handle and lifted the garage door.

The Raggedies were gone. In their place was a new, bright yellow Volkswagen, the new Beetle. It had a Michigan license plate. I shined the light from the flashlight into the car. Hanging from the rear view mirror was something I recognized: a little Raggedy Ann doll. "It's Sarah's, all right," I said. "That's the mascot she used to have in her car in LA."

"Or one just like it," Deborah suggested. "You don't think if she went into the river she'd bother to grab the doll before she escaped from the car, do you?"

"No. I think she ditched the car deliberately. Or someone did it for her. Close the garage door."

The door from the garage to the stairway leading up into the basement above was unlocked. "Sarah?" I called.

No answer.

It had been years since I was in the basement of the cottage. The carcass of a canoe Harold and I had rescued off the beach but never repaired was still there. I remembered what a difficult time we'd had getting it in. Must have been a hundred years ago. Now there were empty shipping cartons and packing popcorn on the floor, signs that Sarah's collection was infecting this place, too. I wondered how long before the cottage would fill up with the trash from Sarah's dolls.

"Sarah?"

The cottage was dead quiet. If Sarah was really there, what if someone had got to her before us? I kept the beam of the flashlight on the floor, afraid that at any moment I would discover a corpse. The blinds were all drawn as before. There was nobody and no body on the ground floor. The Raggedies had taken over. As they had been in Los Angeles, the dolls were everywhere, big ones, small ones, most in their little aprons with their dead eyes staring at nothing at all.

Deborah stumbled on a chair. "Why don't you put on a light?"

"If someone's watching the house I don't want them to know we're here." I turned the beam of the flashlight to guide Deborah.

"Maybe she's be upstairs," I said. "There are three bedrooms." I mounted the stairs and called again, "Sarah?"

A comical figure appeared at the top of the stairs.

"Sarah!" I gasped, much relieved. For days of fruitless searching I'd had a growing apprehension that my sister was dead. She looked the same as when I had seen her last at LAX, the hair in pigtails, the Raggedy Ann apron, the funny red and white striped stockings.

"Adam." She gave me an innocent smile that made me wonder if she wasn't going senile. At least she did recognize my wife. "And you're Deborah. Harold said you'd show up sooner or later."

"If we didn't, I'm afraid someone else would. In fact, they might yet. That's why we're here. Now maybe you should explain how you got there and why your car ended up in the Los Angeles River."

"Come on up," Sarah said, and led us to one of the bedrooms.

She had converted it to an office. The cottage with its three bedrooms and spacious living and dining room downstairs was three times the size of her cramped apartment in LA, but it would not take her long to fill it up with stuff. So far, she still had space. She had piled dolls on the bed, but you could actually see the top of the desk where she had set up her computer.

I recognized the web page. "You're on e-Bay. That's how we found you," I said. "So why did you move?"

"I think Harold got tired of paying my rent. He told me it would be safer here and I'd have more room for the collection."

I had suspected Harold was giving her a subsidy to keep her from being a homeless bag lady. "Safer from what?"

Sarah shrugged. "Safer. I told him I was afraid Schmuel wanted to steal the dolls. What does he know about Raggedy Ann?" She picked up one of the dolls from the floor and hugged it. "She's my sweetheart."

I moved some dolls aside and sat on the bed. "How did your car get into the river?"

"I pushed it. Harold said that with Sadie's money I could buy a new one."

"We saw it," Deborah said as she sat down beside me. "Very nice."

"They didn't have my old color. I liked the orange."

I had made that trip out to LA for nothing. It was all a ruse. "So Harold knew all the time that you were here and didn't tell me."

Sarah gave me a condescending smile. "Harold says you're too honest. You'd tell."

"Did he tell you that Millie got hit by a car and that cousin Arthur and his sister Miriam are dead?"

Sarah was shocked and sat down at the desk. "No."

Deborah came to my defense. "Then maybe Harold doesn't trust you, either. We just came from Arthur and Miriam's funerals. Maybe Harold's afraid you'd send a condolence card."

"That's terrible," Sarah said.

I couldn't tell what Sarah thought was terrible, the deaths of our cousins or that Harold didn't trust her. "I don't think Harold would go to all this trouble just because you were afraid Schmuel would steal your dolls. He must have some ulterior motive."

Deborah had picked up a Raggedy Andy and traced the stenciled "I love you" with her finger. "Maybe Harold's after Sadie's money. If his clients are dead beats, maybe he's broke."

"No way," I said. "He's in control of the trust. If he wanted the money he could embezzle it."

We didn't get to find out-- not then. I heard the sound of breaking glass downstairs.

We all rushed the bedroom door. Looking back on it now, we must have been a comical sight. Three adults, all clutching Raggedy Ann dolls, like we were having a play session.

A voice called from the bottom of the stairs. "Hold it right there. I'm coming up."

She was still wearing the black dress. No veil. She had changed out of the high heel shoes into sneakers. It was Sylvia.

"You followed us," Deborah said.

"How else would I find the place? I've never been here before. Leaving your car out in front helped, but I had to break in the kitchen door. Now back up and sit down, all of you."

The gun in her hand looked familiar. "That Jake's?"

Sylvia's makeup needed rebuilding. She was meticulous about her face and now I could see why. She looked older. Goes to show what that Chicago freeway driving in the dark can do to you. Her smile was twisted. She waved the pistol. "Thanks for leaving it."

Was she alone, I wondered? Three against one was good odds. If we rushed her at the same time she probably couldn't get off more than one wild shot. "Where's Schmuel?"

"Schmuel the schmuck?" She had picked up some Yiddish after all. "Still at Jake's. I told him I'd be right back. He doesn't know anything about this."

I figured it out. "If he doesn't know anything about the murders, even if you're caught for killing us he can inherit the million bucks from Sadie's estate."

Sylvia hissed like a mean cat. "I'm not going to be caught."

"Maybe not," I said. "Then if you haven't spent the money already you can divorce him for half under the California community property law."

Sylvia nodded. "You're smarter than you look, Adam."

"You gonna kill us, too? Couldn't you just ask VISA to boost your credit line?"

"Very funny, Adam. You always were a card. I give you credit for that."

I pretended to laugh. "A credit card. Great pun, Sylvia. You missed your calling. You should have been a comedian. So what are you going to do, kill all of us? What about Jake and Harold?"

"I'll get to them, too. That's one thing you won't have to worry about, because you'll all be dead. Maybe you should have a fire like Arthur. These dolls look pretty flammable to me. Who wants to be first? Any volunteers?" She aimed the gun alternately at each of us.

Funny how much bigger a gun looks when it's pointed at you. I remembered an old trick I saw in a movie once. I stood up, ready to rush her. "You forgot the safety."

"Nice try, Adam." This time she pointed the gun at me and pulled the trigger. Click.

I remembered Jake's firearm instructions. "I took the bullets out," I lied. "Even if you had any, you have to pull the slide back first." Oops. I shouldn't have said that.

Sylvia chambered a round and aimed at Sarah.

Sarah, terrified, tried to hide behind her doll. "Don't shoot Raggedy!"

Sylvia has no respect for the value of a collector's doll. The little .32 made a very loud popping sound and Sarah screamed. A hole had appeared in the chest of the Raggedy Andy. Behind the doll, a hole appeared in Sarah, shattering her left collar bone. Luckily, it missed her neck.

"Doll attack!" I shouted, and started pelting Sylvia with dolls, hoping to get her off balance so she couldn't take good aim at anyone. Deborah got the idea and starting throwing dolls, too.

Involuntarily Sylvia stepped back. Her second shot went wild. Then there was another, louder than the first two. This one sounded like a cannon going off. Sylvia spun around, the little pistol flying through the air. Then, as if someone had yanked the legs out from under her, she was down.

Deborah went for the fallen pistol and I charged across the room to immobilize Sylvia. There was no need. Where her right shoulder had been there was now a bloody mass of blood, flesh and bone splinters. Her eyes were glazed and she was going into shock.

I had never seen a real gun shot wound before. I didn't realize how big a hole a bullet made on its way out.

Sarah was whimpering and crying. She was holding the doll, looking at the hole in it. "You shot Raggedy Andy. Right through the heart, too." She looked across the room at me on the floor tending to Sylvia. "You shot me, too," Sarah said, and fainted.

A voice in the hall said, "She'll live." It was Jake. "Sorry, Adam. I knew when she took off after you what she had in mind. I'm really very sorry. This is all my fault."

Deborah found the bathroom and fetched some towels for a compress to bind over Sylvia's shoulder to slow the bleeding. Sarah seemed not to be badly hurt, though getting shot in any part of the body is not my idea of a good night on the town.

I asked Jake, "How is it your fault?"

"For giving her that contract number. I didn't think she was serious. I thought she was only making conversation. Where's the phone?"

"By the computer, I guess."

Jake went to the desk, found the phone, swore. "Sarah's on line again." He turned off Sarah's computer, dialed a long number. After awhile he said something like, "This is paper boy. I believe your associate had a contract with a certain mutual friend of ours in Los Angeles. Tell him the job is canceled. Someone else did it for him."

"Long distance?" I asked.

Jake gave me a look like "in your dreams" and said, "Everybody's got 800 numbers now. No charge." Then he dialed 911.

Deborah waited on the road for the ambulance and the Michigan State police to arrive. The ambulance came first. The paramedics took Sylvia down on a gurney. By then Sarah had come to and could walk with assistance. She insisted on taking the wounded Raggedy Andy with her and demanded a bandage for the doll.

The state police wouldn't let us follow Sylvia and Sarah to the hospital, but took us to police headquarters. We were to give statements.

I realized that if Jake had shot Sylvia more than once, it could have been murder. Under the circumstances, he had intervened to save our lives. That's the story I stuck to. I hoped he wouldn't be charged. I didn't know if Jake violated any laws transporting a concealed weapon from Illinois, across northern Indiana into Michigan.

After taking our statements the state police released Deborah and me. As for Jake... a funny thing happened. Jake gave the state police a Chicago number to call and they released him, too. Whether or not Jake was charged for shooting Sylvia was up to the prosecutor's discretion.

What kind of connections did Jake have with the Chicago police? It's the kind of question you don't ask if you don't want an evasive answer or a lie.

I supposed that when Sylvia regained consciousness the police did their Miranda card thing and arrested her for attempted murder and home invasion, both felonies. Sylvia is looking at big time in the women's prison. The police put a guard on her at the hospital in Benton Harbor so she wouldn't escape. I didn't think escape was likely, considering that she probably would never be able to use her right arm again.

It was the middle of the night before we got back to Michiana Shores for a few hours sleep. We persuaded Jake not to drive back to Chicago until the next day. Like any good husband, before turning in Jake phoned home to tell Cindy what happened. Schmuel was sleeping in their guest room. Jake told Cindy, "When he wakes up tell him his shicksa wife is in the hospital and will go to jail for attempted murder."

I didn't miss the pejorative Yiddish. Killing all the relatives for money was not something for a nice Jewish girl even if she was married to a Gold and was hooked on the shopping thing.

Deborah moved dolls off the beds in the spare bedroom.

Jake made space among the dolls on the bed in Sarah's office. He's a little guy. Seeing him surrounded by Raggedy Anns I couldn't resist tucking him in. After all, he had saved our lives. He deserved special treatment. I wondered what I should cook him for breakfast. "Want me to read you a story?"

Jake cocked an eye at me. "You nuts?"

"How about Raggedy Andy defeats the wicked witch of the west?"

"Make that wicked bitch," he said and closed his eyes.

43.

The next morning Deborah and I decided to wait for Schmuel to take the South Shore commuter train in from Chicago so he could pick up the rented Neon and then drive to the hospital in Benton Harbor. Sarah's kitchen was well stocked, so I made Jake my version of the Denny's grand slam breakfast, scrambled eggs, hash browns, turkey sausage, and strong coffee.

I didn't know if the prosecutor would offer Sylvia a plea bargain to avoid the expense of a trial or if he had political ambitions and would make an example of her. Either way, she faced hard time in the slammer. If there was a proven connection to Arthur's and Miriam's deaths she'd be up for conspiracy and murder one as they say on TV.

Deborah and I sent Jake on his way. Deborah canceled her appointments for the day. As soon as she could be released from the hospital, we'd get Sarah and bring her and the wounded doll back to the lake.

I phoned Harold at his office in Indianapolis to give him the news.

As usual he was eating at his desk and talking with his mouth full. I asked, "Don't you ever go out to eat? What is it this time?"

"It's my routine," Harold wheezed. "Every day the same thing. Four jelly donuts and coffee for breakfast, a foot long sub for lunch. Then my wife and I eat out for supper. She doesn't like to cook."

No wonder he was so fat. I told him about Sylvia, Sarah's wounded shoulder. Jake's gun. The whole story.

Harold thought it was funny. "I knew something like this would happen when I talked Sarah into ditching her car and moving to the lake."

"It was all your idea, you prick. You wanted to see what the cousins would do for a million dollars."

"I was just jerking their chain." Harold laughed again. "It's not a million dollars."

"What?" Not that I had visions of being a millionaire if I were the last survivor. Sarah was the youngest. Unless she got blood poisoning or something from that gun shot, she'd outlive all of us. "You said it was a million."

Harold paused. I could hear him gulping coffee. "Adam, you remember the conversation when you were all at Sadie's Shiva reception? I didn't say Sadie left one million dollars. I said, 'Would you believe a million.' It's only four hundred thousand."

I thought of the consequences he had precipitated. "What a rotten thing to do. It's the Gold chromosome at work. And you call yourself a Rottman."

"Blood will tell," Harold said, snickering. "And one other thing. I lied about the tontine. There is no tontine. When Sarah passes on, the trust is divided equally among the cousins, their heirs and assigns."

I couldn't think of anything to say, I was so appalled.

Harold was laughing again. "It was all a joke," he said, his mouth full of jelly donut. Then silence.

"Harold?"

I heard the phone thumping and odd noises from Harold's office. Then someone hung up.

I tried calling back, but the line was busy.

"It was all a joke," I told Deborah. "Not one million dollars. And no tontine."

Deborah understood. "The Gold chromosome. Someone ought to play a trick like that on Harold. See how he feels about it."

It wasn't necessary. When I tried calling back a few minutes later Harold's paralegal secretary answered. She was stressed and shaken. My brother had choked on a piece of donut, she said. She tried to give him the Heimlich maneuver, but he was so fat she had a hard time trying. You only have about a minute to do the Heimlich grip to dislodge food caught in someone's throat.

Eventually his secretary did succeed, got the bit of food dislodged, but the strain on Harold's heart was too great. He had a heart attack. I had to conclude that what goes around comes around. He was my brother, but he deserved it.

You know what Schmuel said when we picked him up at the South Shore station in Michigan City and told him the story? He said, "Sylvia did it all for me."

"No she didn't," I told him. "She did it for herself."

He followed us in the Neon to Benton Harbor where we visited Sarah. She was enjoying herself. She and the bandaged Raggedy Andy doll were sitting up in the hospital bed watching Sesame Street on the television. She'll be OK. Harold's widow says she can stay in the lake cottage as long as she likes.

Another funeral. I hope there won't be another Gold funeral for a long time to come. As for Sadie's money, I really don't care.

If you enjoyed *The Gold Chromosome*, you may like another of Harley's funny mysteries, *The Lollipop Murder*. Here's a sample:

One

"You've got a letter from your publisher," Devra said the moment Luther S— walked in through the door of their studio apartment in Portland, Oregon. What with Devra's student loan still not paid off, even with both of them working, a studio was all they could afford. It was similar to living in a motel room, not much unlike the temporary quarters otherwise homeless families were shunted into to keep them off the streets. The best Luther could do in the way of an academic job at Portland State University was an adjunct position, professorspeak for part time work, no benefits, large classes, no tenure and little hope.

At least an adjunct position left Luther time to polish that academic novel he'd used as a thesis at the University of Iowa writing program. Thanks to his University of Iowa roommate Charlie Broadbottom he had actually found a publisher. Charlie was a British transplant who used his accent to charm the University of Iowa coeds. He could be induced to imitate the BBC, an accent no known Brit outside of broadcasting ever affected. Besides being effective with girls, it helped him land a job with *Publishers' Journal*.

Broadbottom had steered Luther to an obscure publisher, Ira Ripov, who had actually taken him on for his stable of authors. Stroke of luck, sort of. It helped to have connections.

The result was Luther had a so-called debut novel, *Tracking Tenure*. Besides nearly crying with joy when he got his six author's copies, the book gave him a bit of hope. Bppks made money, right? He and Devra needed some extra income. At first the book had attracted a couple of reviews in publications but, though favorable, no fat royalties were forthcoming.

Being a so-called local author was enough to get him an appearance in the bowels of Annie Bloom's bookstore in Multnomah Village, but not at Powell's which would have been a real plum. Powell's was the largest independent bookstore on the West Coast if not the entire United States, and had a steady stream of top authors doing readings and signings for as many as a hundred devoted onlookers. Luther S-- was not in that class.

Ira Ripov had not paid an advance, Luther being a neophyte author, nor did he finance a book tour. The best Luther could arrange, besides the appearance at Annie Bloom's before twelve mildly curious onlookers, were a couple of appearances at independent bookstores on the Oregon coast, namely at Cannon Beach and Newport. That was that. What did he sell? A dozen copies? He knew the royalties, if Ripov ever paid him, wouldn't cover the cost of the gas to drive to the Oregon Coast in their aging Toyota, not to mention the value of his time on a per hour basis, which amounted to nothing. He was beginning to lose hope.

Devra had reminded him that even if he didn't sell many copies of *Tracking Tenure*, he was raising his profile from being a totally unknown author to a small blip on the literary screen in Oregon. The published title helped his resume as an academic and might help him land a real, full time, tenure track teaching job, not just piecework, paid per course taught.

Luther hadn't heard from Ira Ripov in weeks and had been warned by pal Charlie at *Publishers' Journal* that publishers didn't like to be pestered by authors who expected instant riches. Today's mail from Ripov, addressed by hand in formal copperplate on an announcement-style envelope, was a welcome surprise which he held in suspense. "Do you think it's a royalty check?"

Devra rolled her eyes. Devra didn't wear makeup and was blessed with the flawless skin of a twelve year old. She was still wearing her uniform from the VA hospital where she was a professional vampire, the med techs' inside joke about doing hundreds of blood draws from the pale, withered arms of disabled vets, no take home samples, please. Eventually she hoped to complete her nurse's training at OHSU, Oregon Health Sciences University, and be an RN. "Doesn't look like it. Checks come in number ten envelopes with windows. This one is almost square, fancy paper, looks like an invitation."

It was.

The formal invitation was printed on cream colored stock with a ragged edge.

You are invited
to attend the
First Annual Lollipop Awards Presentation
At the Miami Book Fair
August 10. Reception at 7:00 PM Dress casual.
Overnight accommodations on board
the M/Y Lollipop
Crab Cake Marina, Biscayne Bay, Miami, Florida
RSVP

About Harley L. Sachs:

Though born in Chicago and raised in Indiana, Harley L. Sachs considers himself an international, having lived in Germany, Sweden, Scotland, and Denmark. He earned a degree in English at Indiana University, then served in the US Army in Germany. After getting his Master's degree at I.U. he returned to Europe and worked under cover for several years. He met and married Ulla in Stockholm, Sweden and they spent a year's honeymoon in a Scottish castle. Returning to the USA, Sachs taught English briefly at Southern Illinois University then moved to Michigan Technological University in the Upper Peninsula where he and his wife raised three daughters. He took early retirement and now lives in Portland, Oregon.

Harley L. Sachs is the author of many novels, short stories, magazine articles and newspaper columns. His short stories have been broadcast on the BBC World Service short wave and on Oregon Public Radio's Golden Hours

Here's a list of books by Harley L. Sachs:

MYSTERY NOVELS

The Mystery Club Series

THE MYSTERY CLUB SOLVES A MURDER

First and most popular of the Mystery Club series. Mary Higgins finds the body of Dora Reed on the roof of the Plaza retirement building, notifies the police, then tells the Mystery Club. They assume several suspects: the manager of the Plaza, Dora's son Donald, or a Plaza employee. Dora's husband, Ed Sutherland, is in Hawaii on board the yacht Miss Chief with an all girl crew. Carrying on their own investigation, the Mystery Club finally suspects Sutherland, though he seems to have a perfect alibi. If they can prove it to their satisfaction, will a court ever convict him-- if he can be found somewhere in the Pacific?

THE MYSTERY CLUB AND THE DEAD DOCTOR

Second in the Mystery Club series. The Mystery Club consists of five elderly women who live at the Rose Plaza and discuss mysteries written by women. The Mystery Club ladies have no idea of the consequences when Viola Cartwright, their blind member, asks them to go over her Medicare bills. That leads to suspicion about the identity of her personal assistant, Dorothy Anderson, who turns out to be using a stolen identity. Viola's doctor runs a phony clinic owned by a member of the Russian Mafia. Soon the investigation of Medicare bills leads to murder and tragedy, stopped only by the courage of Mary Higgins.

THE MYSTERY CLUB AND THE HIDDEN WITNESS

Third in the Mystery Club series. The ladies of the Mystery Club discover one of the residents is a crook under WITSEC, the witness protection program. He apparently keeps dipping into the employee gift fund. The Mystery Club bands together to track down the missing money, but what they discover is danger.

THE MYSTERY CLUB AND THE SERIAL WIDOW

Fourth in the Mystery Club series. Caroline Kostinsky, new resident at the Rose Plaza, is a widow four times over and she's looking for a fifth husband in retired General Hardcastle, but when drunk she says she killed all of her husbands. Except for her confession, there's no evidence. Now what?

DELIVER ME FROM EVIL

Responding to a posted invitation for new members for the Mystery Club, Judge Ira Kahane and Ursula Besette show up. Ursula, at a turning point in her life as a new Rose Plaza resident, is interested in Wicca and Kabala. Roberta Nelson believes one should not suffer a witch to live. Judge Kahane tries to lead Ursula on the right path, but there is conflict and tragedy coming.

WHITE SLAVE

Sequel to *The Mystery Club Solves a Murder.* The appearance of Ed Sutherland's gold bracelet in a Portland pawn shop revives retired detective Casey's interest in the cold case. He doesn't know that Sutherland has been picked up and is a slave on a Korean fishing boat. Sutherland, penniless, .without clothes or identification, is stranded in New Zealand. Can he find his way back to Portland and be somehow redeemed or face a death sentence for first degree murder?

The Irwin Glass Series

BETRAYAL

Prequel to *Retribution.* Irwin Glass, BA in Russian, MA in International Relations, has a promising career in the Foreign Service in Moscow until he is snared in a classic "honey pot" seduction. He's young and naïve, honest, always wants to do the right thing, but at every turn he is betrayed. The incident in Moscow destroys his career. He is accused of being a paid Soviet agent and is pursued by the consequences of his encounter with the KGB twenty years later. Some enemies never let go

RETRIBUTION

Sequel to *Betrayal.* Newly married to Ivy Hartshorn, Irwin Glass gets a dunning letter from the IRS for taxes on interest at the Washington, DC account he didn't think he had. It's a joint account with his missing birth daughter and the balance is huge. Assuming it's money Katya's KGB father of record, Vladimir Putinsky (now Putin) deposited for her living expenses, Irwin moves it to force her to contact him. But Ivy warns him that he is laundering money and the people it belongs to will come after him. Irwin's complicated life is catching up with him, but this time he will find retribution.

BURNT OUT

Irwin Glass is approached by FBI Agent Wilkins who asks for Irwin's lists of foreign students. Not satisfied he wants more and is looking for potential terrorists among the Moslem students. Gradually Irwin is sucked into the role of FBI informant on the Michigan Institute of Technology's Muslim Students' Association and the results are tragic.

THE IRWIN GLASS TRILOGY

All three Irwin Glass books in one package deal. The Irwin Glass Trilogy combines all three of the Irwin Glass Mysteries: "Betrayal," "Retribution," and "Burnt Out," following the chaotic career of Irwin Glass who began, in "Betrayal," as a state department clerk in Moscow only to be caught in a classic honey pot seduction. Betrayed at every turn, he was sent back to the United States in disgrace to try to start a new life. No such luck. His teaching career is upturned by the revelation that the Moscow seduction had a consequence in the form of a beautiful student Katya who claims to be his daughter. In "Retribution," Irwin's KGB nemesis is in the

United States seeking political asylum, but in fact is fleeing the Russian Mafia with Irwin as quarry. After "Retribution," Irwin thinks he is home free of all that intrigue, but the local FBI agent has a hold on him and wants information about potential terrorists among Irwin's students at Michigan Institute of Technology. There are risks to being a reluctant FBI informant, and Irwin's reports may be misconstrued with tragic results. What Irwin and his wife really want is a normal life, but his mysterious Russian birth daughter Katya remains an enigma. Is she or isn't she?

Other Mysteries

MURDER BY MAIL

German exchange student Klaus Hitz is more interested in making money than in asking questions about his work assignment. He doesn't know that the industrialist father of his punk girl friend is using him in a terrorist conspiracy to kill everyone in the United States with a mass mailing of a scratch and sniff virus. The plot begins to unravel when a Polish nurse brings blood samples from Libya and alerts a CIA agent. While the CIA and FBI track down the terrorists, Klaus Hitz gradually figures it out. How can he avoid being murdered or imprisoned for being naive?

MURDER IN THE KEWEENAW

CIA agent recovering from Post traumatic Stress after failed missions in Finland and a divorce is fishing in Lake Superior when he snags a corpse. He thinks he has seen the girl before and his attempt to identify her leads him to a ring of deadly pornographers. It almost costs him his own life.

CONSPIRACY!

Technical writer Tom Godot can't believe his luck when CONSPIRACY!, the book he has co-written with the elusive Harold Stevenson, is a hit. The book details a plot to hijack communication satellites. As Tom crosses the country on his book tour, he is disturbed by people interested in early drafts and dogged by an NSA agent. Communicating by fax with his editor and by encrypted e-mail with the mysterious Stevenson, Tom reaches out in his loneliness to his California girl friend Sylvia Hanson who turns out to be a pivotal figure. There is another conspiracy, and Tom is part of it

THE GOLD CHROMOSOME

When Adam Rottman's childless Aunt Sadie Gold died, the eight cousins learned her estate was in an irrevocable trust, the proceeds going to Adam's sister Sarah while she lives. After Sarah's death, the money would go to the last surviving cousin. It's a fatal tontine Adam's lawyer brother Harold set up. Would the cousins kill each other for one million dollars? Sarah's car is found in the river, but not Sarah. That begins a series of mysterious deaths. Coincidence? Or Murder? Who will be next? Adam and his psychologist wife Deborah must stop the chain before he, too, is eliminated.

BEN ZAKKAI'S COFFIN

Born of a Jewish father and a Catholic mother, Herman Bachrach insists he has no religion, but he is drawn by circumstance into a holocaust vendetta over gold stolen by a Swiss bank from Jewish depositors. Seduced by a woman who calls herself Diana, no last name, Herman is suspected by detective Sheehan to be her murderer. Someone else wants him dead. His Jewish boss provides him with a lawyer, but sends him to Switzerland to finish the job "Diana" started. It's an assignment he can't refuse. The result is an epiphany of identity that changes Herman's life forever.

THE LOLLIPOP MURDER

A warning for wannabe novelists! What happens when a stable of neurotic novelists who live in their pseudonyms and are bound by iron clad contracts are invited aboard their miserly Florida publisher's yacht for the Miami Book Fair only to find that they have no hope of ever earning a dime of royalties for their books? All this as Hurricane Gerta threatens to sink the yacht at the dock. It's grounds for murder

SAM IN LOVE

A coming of age romance for mature young adults. U.S. Army life in Europe in the 1950's was an equivalent of the Grand Tour of the eighteenth century when young men traveled and sowed wild oats. Marty, roommate of Sam Logan, a PFC draftee serving in the US Army in Munich, Germany, says all Sam needs is to get laid. Sam is not a virgin, but has a Midwestern ethic and believes in love. He doesn't know quite what that is. No Casanova, Sam, through a series of tentative encounters, thinks he's found the love of his life.

STOPRAPE.COM

Kerstin Mikkola, a young TV reporter at KDUP in Marquette, Michigan has hopes of a better network job. Her interview with a marine victim or rape might be just the ticket. Her interview about the web site StopRape.com goes viral on U-tube and Kerstin finds herself in the thick of consequences she did not anticipate.

THE ACCIDENTAL COURIER

A romance, road trip, and mystery all in one. Charles Kosko, retired orchard owner from Oregon, decides to take a bus trip in Europe and finds himself involved in a whistle-blower's scheme to discredit an American cell phone company that uses rare earths mined by slaves in the Congo. Unable to speak any foreign language, and without his US passport, he is picked up by a beautiful Israeli woman who says she is his driver. But is he really her prisoner? They are pursued by an African mining engineer, who hopes to intercept the delivery of stolen rare earths,

Harley L. Sachs
SCI-FI AND FANTASY

NEVER TRUST A TALKING HORSE

The narrator of this dystopian novel escapes preventive detention into a world he discovers has gone mad. Hungry, he is told he can eat for free at Lachumba's supper club, only to discover that he might be the main dish. He rescues Iris I. Iris from the ovens and in a series of episodes explores the insane world in search of a livelihood. He gradually realizes why he was incarcerated in the first place, but by then it is too late. His and Iris's roles have been reversed. Arrested, they are given a sadistic sentence which is their final challenge.

THE SEARCH FOR JESSE BRAM

Jesse Bram, the young hero of this metaphysical science fiction adventure, is unaware of his Jewish roots. An Eldre of mixed breed, he is marooned on the post apocalyptic shunned planet URth where technology and books have been destroyed. The URthlings variously view Jesse as a bringer of cargo for the half-breed prefect Hrod, as the reborn Savior by crypto-Christians, and as a link to the past by a remnant of Jews. The Galactic Federation suspects him of treason and he is pursued by an enigmatic Trinian policeman. If Jesse survives, will he be convicted? If acquitted, what next?

SHORT STORIES

THREADS OF THE COVENANT: THE JEWS OF RED JACKET

A collection of twenty-one short stories about Jewish life in small town America centering about two main characters, David Katz, the only Jewish boy in Red Jacket, and Richard Goldman, the only Jewish professor at Copper country Community College. Each story depicts another aspect of what it means to be a Jew in a small town as each character comes to realize his own identity.

MISPLACED PERSONS

Though set in different locales what these stories have in common is a central character who is out of his element, in the wrong place, coming to grips with cultural, generational, or physical displacement. In PROBLEM FOR THE TEACHER an expatriate fumbles for a living; in LIMBO an ex-G.I. is adrift in Copenhagen; in TRIUMPH OF THE WILL a nervous wreck seeks recuperation; in MISCALCULATION a would be tax evader succumbs to his own fears; in THE LIE a drunk gets himself into difficulties, and in THE GIRLS OF FREDERIKSHAVN an old man is trapped by girls looking for action.

YOOPER TALES AND OTHER FUNNY STUFF

Extracted from the massive volume of Sachs's published Essays and Columns: 1992-2011, this collection of stories related to Michigan's Upper Peninsula, known as the UP, home of Yoopers, reveals the truth about snow fleas, ice worms, the humungous fungus (world's largest living thing) and the rigors of winters in the remote north woods. You can also learn how to catch and cook the Mosquito Giganticus and why visitors won't come. Sachs has several awards for his humor.

AHOY! QUARTERDECK!

Originally published as IRMA QUARTERDECK REPORTS but re-released with new illustrations and, in the paperback edition, with sea shanties, this funny book is a series of boating anecdotes about Irma and her bumbling husband Ralph ("I can't believe I lost the anchor") Quarterdeck in their many boating adventures and mishaps. One reviewer says the book is as informative as Chapman's famous manual, but more fun. Readers will find plenty of laughs in this book and at the same time learn a great deal of boating fundamentals.

ANNA-LENA'S TROLL AND OHER STORIES

Each of the three Sachs daughters has a story in this children's book. "Anna-Lena's Troll" explores the nature of trolls, which represent the dark side of human behavior as Anna-Lena's nasty letter to Santa is rewarded by the gift of a nasty troll. "The Return of Baby Suzy" is the true story of Cynthia's worn out doll and its resurrection. "The Stars for Christmas" is the remarkable surprise Belinda got along with her new eye glasses. Other family stories are Christmas related.

NON-FICTION

THE MISADVENTURES OF CPL. SACHS

Adrift through college at Indiana University, author Sachs was drafted at the end of the Korean War. Physically unfit for combat, he was sent to Queer Company for basic training, then by a fluke was shipped out to Germany instead of Korea. Thus began his own version of the traditional Grand Tour.

FREELANCE NONFICTION ARTICLES

This third edition of a monograph on freelance writing first published by the Society for Technical Communication is newly updated. This little manual provides tips for interviewing, article structure, article preparation and submission, photography, and business practice.

CHILLY-CHILLY-BANG—HOW WE FREELANCED THROUGH EUROPE'S COLDEST WINTER IN A VW WITH A KID

Companion piece to *Freelance Nonfiction Articles*. The former is a how to book. This is a "how we did it" memoir. The author knew nothing about Volkswagens when they set off, but as they worked from VW dealer to dealer getting the old Combi fixed, he learned! It's as much a book for VW enthusiasts as it is for writers.

Both FREELANCE NONFICTION ARTICLES and *Chilly-Chilly-BANG! How we Freelanced Through Europe's Coldest Winter in a VW with a Kid* are combined in a double volume, *The Writing Life*.

THE 1957 SACHS ARCTIC EXPEDITION

After military service in Germany the author took the GI Bill to Sweden. With no income in the summer, and not even sure there was a road to the far north, he set off hitchhiking to North Cape, the northernmost point in Europe in search of the midnight sun. Illustrated.

FROM TENT TO CASTLE: MEMOIR OF A YEAR LONG HONEYMOON

Setting off from Stockholm, Sweden on rebuilt one speed bicycles, Harley and Ulla embarked on an open-ended honeymoon with no fixed destination and equipped with a tent, a thin double sleeping bag, a tiny gasoline stove, and $3000. After arriving in Britain, Ulla discovered she was pregnant. Tired of unrelenting rain, they advertised for a cheap place to spend the winter. They were offered the gatehouse to Borthwick Castle outside Edinburgh, Scotland for $25 a month by British author Theo Lang.

"IS"

As Bill Clinton said, "It all depends on what the meaning of "is" is."

A problem we all have is distinguishing between what is real and what is not. This is in fact an age-old question. This volume switches between classical instances of the problem to the author and his psychiatrist and his wife. What is real? That all depends on the meaning of "real."

QUEER COMPANY

Not a gay novel, this is a fictionalized memoir of an experimental basic training unit at the end of the Korean War. All the draftees were physically unfit for combat but the army didn't want to discharge them. Instead they got modified training in a company unfortunately designated Q. In the Army phonetic alphabet Q is Queen, but Q company was called queer. A copy is in the US Army historical archives.

www.ingramcontent.com/pod-product-compliance
Lightning Source LLC
Chambersburg PA
CBHW070028260626
47159CB00005B/1984